M000308356

The Jewish Spy
Hayuta Katzenelson

This book is dedicated to the memory of my dear parents, Rosa and Zvi Friedlander, and my older brother Shlomo, who passed away at the age of 43. It is also dedicated to my beloved brother, Isaac, may he live a long and prosperous life, his wife, Mary, and his children and grandchildren.

My thanks and my love are dedicated to my three sons, Tzachi, Hemi, and Tzvika, their precious wives, Dalit, Yifat, and Ayala, and my dear grandchildren Moran, Shiran, Shira, Talia, Itay, Raz, Abigail and Ariel.

Last but not least, to my dear, beloved husband, Joshua, who supported me during the writing of the book. Thank you.

Hayuta

Producer & International Distributor
eBookPro Publishing
www.ebook-pro.com

The Jewish Spy
Hayuta Katzenelson

Copyright © 2020 Hayuta Katzenelson

All rights reserved; No parts of this book may be reproduced
or transmitted in any form or by any means, electronic or
mechanical, including photocopying, recording, taping, or
by any information retrieval system, without the permission, in writing, of the author.

Contact: tbcarmi@gmail.com

ISBN 9789655751376

THE JEWISH SPY

HAYUTA KATZENELSON

PART ONE: RIVKA

Chapter 1

Rivka's whole body ached with nostalgia, even though her husband and children were with her in her hometown of Nadvorna to celebrate her forty-second birthday.

Her blue eyes were dreaming as she helped her mother, Masha, get seated at the table. How could she leave her parents, who had always supported her, behind? Since her older brother's death at a young age from tuberculosis, she had felt obligated to be especially attentive and acquiesce to their wishes. There was even a sort of guilt she carried as the one who survived. Her parents' sorrow that they wouldn't have grandchildren from their son led her to wed after a brief courtship. *What's the point in putting it off?* echoed in her head after she accepted the proposal. Their three grandchildren comforted them for the death of their son.

The dining table was laden with delicious food. Rex, the black dog belonging to her youngest son, David, hovered around the table, wagging his tail and hoping that a crumb would fall near him. With a heavy heart, Rivka placed the platters and serving bowls on the mahogany dining table that filled the kitchen area. The dishes provided splashes of color on the table: orange from the carrots and sweet potatoes in the tzimmes, purple from the plums in the compote and the raisins in the sweet kugel that she'd prepared with the children. They'd helped make the kugel, but they loved the fried kreplach and the fried potato pancakes more. She would miss the frequent arguments with the children about how much they ate, as they were too thin for her liking.

Her eyes scanned the table with unexpected emotion. It had been crafted carefully — as a piece of furniture created by a young artist should be. The table had been carved by hand, by Yaakov, her husband. She was filled with sorrow at the idea that the table would soon be orphaned. Children would not be gathered around it, and it would probably be separated from its creator forever. She caressed the carvings on the corner next to her and thought to herself, *this was the first piece of furniture that Yaakov made for us.*

The atmosphere was unbearable. The separation was about to hit each and every one of them. Yaakov insisted that to save the children they had to leave Poland despite his wife's protests. She believed that the rumors about German pogroms were just that —rumors — and that no harm would come to them.

***

Yaakov had worked in her father's carpentry workshop from the day they got married. Every morning he would arrive with a smile. Yaakov loved the feel of the wood and the way it responded to the carving instruments in his capable hands. For him, every piece of furniture that left the workshop was a one-of-a-kind piece of art.

"Do you want some tea?" Shlomo would ask each morning while boiling water.

"No, thank you," Yaakov replied every morning, always eager to get started with his work.

Then Shlomo would burst into full persuasion. "Why not?" he argued every morning, and poor Yaakov would always smile and give in.

His father-in-law would hand him a cup of tea with lemon and a special dish for the sugar cubes. They would sit and drink tea, melting the sugar cubes in their mouths with every sip. Only the sound of the cups and the sips was heard. A peaceful brotherhood of men.

Shlomo spread his wings a little over Yaakov because, while his daughter's husband could not replace his lost son, the older man was comforted by his presence.

After the tea worked to warm their bones from the outside cold, they would begin their work. The first table Yaakov made, he dedicated to his wife and his future descendants. Shlomo had watched the efforts of his apprentice, the intensity with which he worked, and urged him to make the mahogany table for his family. A sense of joy and love of creativity bubbled in Yaakov's veins with each tap of the chisel, with each stroke of the plane. He brought the table to Rivka, and it made her happy. He needed nothing more.

She recalled the day the table arrived and she had tried to figure out how best to place it in their kitchen. The table was a little long and blocked the cooking area. They found a solution by setting it against the wall bordering the living room. Their house was cozy and carefully decorated. Rivka kept it bright with flowers from their little garden displayed on the beautiful table.

Just as Yaakov did in the carpentry shop, at home Rivka devoted her days to work. She learned to sew from her mother, and made pretty blue curtains, the color of her eyes, for their humble home. Having his own home gave Yaakov great pride.

In the first years of their marriage, Rivka devoted herself to homemaking. It was only after their three children were in school that she was persuaded to gather information for the Jewish underground; but these activities she kept a secret from her family so as not to endanger them.

Rakhel was their first child. She was the spitting image of her mother. Her eyes were blue and her hair was fair. Masha helped Rivka raise the child — her first grandchild. Oh, how happy she was! She invested all her energy in the little girl. She babbled at her in various languages, a mixture of all the tongues she knew. A phrase in Yiddish seasoned with a touch of Polish, and for good measure she taught her phrases in

English and German.

Masha had acquired these languages when her mother worked as a dentist in Vienna. She had chosen to study languages spoken more widely than Austrian and Gothic German, although she spoke those as well.

Rakhel was very attached to Masha. When her brothers were born, Rakhel found herself spending a considerable amount of time at her grandmother's house while her mother took care of the little boys. When they were old enough, Laibel and David would study in the *cheder*. And she, in her grandmother's house, was the center of attention. When she reached school age, Rakhel chose to study at her grandmother's. She received instruction in arithmetic, history, Judaism, and languages. When she wasn't gaining book knowledge, she worked side by side with Masha becoming skilled in sewing, cooking, and baking.

When Rakhel was at home with her mother, they would enjoy each other's company baking breads, pastries, and other sweets. But for Yaakov, as a special treat, Rivka would prepare his favorite kugel like he had at his father's house.

Rivka's mind traveled back to the present, and her gaze returned to the dining table. Yaakov was endlessly chewing the kugel she had made for him. His eyes were distant, and it was clear he was unable to swallow: Some anger he was holding back had rendered the muscles in his throat useless. The noise of plates against the table, forks chiming on the porcelain, chewing mouths, and slurping of compote sauce filled the air — David had not yet learned how to eat politely.

Rivka felt frozen inside. She had locked the pain she knew was coming in a box inside her heart and refused to feel it prematurely. The bustle of eating was white noise in the background of her thoughts. She caught a glimpse of David feeding Rex some treats from the table. She turned a blind eye; she had no energy to reprimand this time around. Nevertheless, he would have to learn courtesy and manners from his father, now that she wouldn't be there to remind him.

Shlomo sat at the table watching his grandchildren, his endless heartache for his absent son reflected on his face. That sorrow was compounded by the thought that he and his wife might never see their grandchildren again. That same grief was in Masha's eyes despite her attempts to smile. Rivka knew it well. Since her brother's death, she'd been very attuned to her mother's forlorn stares. The laughter of the grandchildren, the simple delight of children enjoying their favorite food, could always put a smile on her lips. *What will my mother do without them?* Rivka asked herself. *What would I do?* The thought hung there unfinished. She blinked and looked at the first thing her eyes settled on. The laundry. It had been three days since she folded laundry. Her own laundry.

The children's clothes had been already packed. Yaakov's had been pressed. She had almost caressed them with the iron when getting their suitcases ready. Her beautiful daughter, Rakhel, seventeen years old, with her smooth hair and blue eyes. *Certainly, soon she'll find herself a young man,* she'd thought. *Perhaps I not live to see my grandchildren*, the thought had curled up like a vapor among the clothes. *Well, it's too early to think about it*. When that idea had come to her, she shook a shirt vigorously as if shaking the thought out if it. Laibel, her son, was almost a man at fourteen, and seven-year-old David was just a boy. She was hoping that they would integrate quickly, make new friends, and adapt to the new language in distant America.

Oh, how far away America was. A tough journey in the belly of a ship was what separated Europe from America. A journey that would not be easy and would be full of turmoil.

She tried to smile, to store inside the last moments with her parents and her children all together. She even surrendered to the pleading in Rex's eyes for the fragrant pancake still left on the plate.

Chapter 2

"How can you break up the family so easily?" A lump formed in Yaakov's throat as he gave Rivka his piece of mind. *Not easily!* Rivka replied in her head. Not a word crossed her lips.

He had never felt so distant from his wife, as if she were on the other side of an unknown barricade and not his wife any longer. And yet he tried to hold on to her and their family with all his heart. They were his life.

"You are so selfish!" He broke down in tears. "What crime did your children commit? They need you, especially in a strange and unfamiliar place. They will grow up resenting you for this. And maybe won't even be able to forgive you. I know I will have a hard time doing so."

"I pray that they will be able to forgive me," she replied, and in her mind she continued her response to him. *If they only knew, if you only knew ... my fate is linked to all the Jews and the State of Israel whose creation I am helping to bring about. If only I could tell you, I'm sure you'd understand!*

The drop that meandered down his cheek left a white salt

trail. *He doesn't drink enough water*, Rivka thought anxiously, as if the amount of water Yaakov drank was the most important thing she had to think about, before Yaakov's voice penetrated her thoughts.

"The German Reich is knocking on our door; this is the reality, Rivka. He is provoking the European countries, and those imbeciles are keeping silent! It's all because of the bruised egos of the Germans, I tell you. The Brits and the French forced them to pay for the ravages of the war, and look how now he plays tricks on them."

Rivka did not contest him. Hitler spoke repeatedly about the aspirations of Nazism for a new order in Europe.

Yaakov continued with intensity. "Hitler invaded the right bank of the Rhine even though it was declared a demilitarized zone! These uber-clever ones over there in France and Britain do not respond. Maybe they think it's all far away from them, but they are wrong. Keeping quiet! I know, they think that if they don't respond they will prevent a war, but it's the opposite! And what's more, they are trying to appease Hitler. But I am telling you, they cannot be more wrong! Even Austria was annexed to Germany, and these politicians, the Brits and the French still do not get involved! I am telling you, they are making a mistake. This German character isn't behaving like they thought he would. Even a child needs limits, otherwise he'll never stop. Obsequious weaklings! You hear me, Rivka? We must get out of here!"

Rivka looked at him, her eyes cloudy, and she knew inside

that he was right. She just sat and listened.

"My sister Hannah will take care of us: an apartment, a job, all we need."

Rivka's every muscle went rigid. Although she had not yet said a word, Yaakov already knew what she was thinking. She did not want to go. Couldn't go.

"I do not understand you!" he called out desperately. "How do you not understand that this is a critical time? An opportunity that will not come again. You might not be able to leave later." He tried to speak to her heart. Plead, really.

Rivka sat quietly as Yaakov calmed a little, and then she slowly said, "How do you not see my parents' plight? They are in need of care. Physically. And mentally. I cannot bear the thought of them not surviving the trip. And in their final days to change countries? Languages? They draw strength from the four walls of their home and their land."

A look of incomprehension came over Yaakov's face. Her work for the Jewish underground she could not share with him. And there was another thing she didn't tell him: Every Friday before Shabbat, her parents visited the cemetery with a bouquet of flowers they picked from their garden, and they would tell her brother about all that had happened to them during the week. This little ritual would give them peace until their next visit. The thought that they would be forced to abandon the weekly meeting with their son at his grave wouldn't give her rest.

The more Yaakov talked, the more she felt herself

burrowing deeper and deeper into the soft red wool scarf her mother had knitted for her. She was torn beyond all expression. She loved her children dearly. However, her automatic response in conflicts such as this was a reluctant withdrawal and the inability to explain or defend herself. Anger flooded her with each of Yaakov's stabbing words, until she chose not to answer him and to just wrap herself up in her shawl.

And she? Where was she in all this? She felt she had to try to remember who she was before she got married and gave birth. Did she really love Yaakov? She cared for him, certainly. *What is there beyond the caring*, she asked herself. She felt her mind was digging a trench for her to hide in.

When Yaakov tried to talk to her heart softly, her shawl slid ever so slightly off her shoulder. Consumed with guilt about her parents and Yaakov, but firmly believing she couldn't share the main reason for staying behind, she felt trapped. She mustn't say a thing. "It should have been me, not my brother," she finally said.

Yaakov looked up at Rivka. "Will you let the past manage your life forever? You were always the spoiled one in your family, and that's how you still are," he snapped.

"My parents preferred me over my brother all these years, and it seems that fate or God preferred me too. And now that I am their only child, how could I disappoint them? Is it not enough that their grandchildren will leave them?" Her pain hung at the end of her sentence like a surfer on the question mark trying not to fall off. "You know how fragile they are.

Their faces — full of wrinkles. Every wrinkle earned with hard work, sweat, sorrow, and joy," she whispered. "Remember how happy they were when our children were born? With every child their faces lit up! Masha took Laibel in her arms when he was born. Through her gladness, I watched her eyes mist over. A mikveh of longing. How many tears she shed over her dead son!" Rivka also wiped away a tear, remembering that moment of bliss mixed with yearning.

"Rivka ..." Yaakov answered then said no more.

***

David, unlike Laibel, resembled Yaakov. Emotional, with a stubborn set to his face and eyes like brown honey. David was the youngest, and his black German shepherd Rex was like a little brother to him. A compliant playmate he could guide and instruct. The one he could order around, run wild with.

When David was very little he would chase Rex with a stick, and Rivka would stand between them as a barrier, trying to teach him patience and compassion for animals. Rex seemed to look at her with thanks and wagged his tail as a sign of his love. Each time she stepped into the room, he'd bark in her direction happily, jumping around and almost knocking her over as he grew. Scolding did nothing to dissuade him from this behavior, so Rivka always surrendered. She would stare into his dark brown eyes, deeper even than David's, and ruffle his shiny black fur, stroking his neck under his muzzle. Rex did not like being patted on his head, and he moved away when anyone tried. Rex knew how to give his paw when they said "hand," to retrieve a ball, to identify specific sounds, and to distinguish between friends and foes when visitors came to call.

As David grew, Rex had become his full-time companion. They would walk in the woods with Rex tight to David's right leg, not daring to walk faster than his master. When David stopped, Rex also stopped. If David stood stationary, Rex sat patiently and waited. Only when David said, "Free," did he dare to sniff around and frolic, do his business and cover it up, snuffle for mushrooms, chase small rodents, and scare cats to the treetops.

Once, on a day of this sort of mischief in the forest, Rex froze without warning and his ears straightened and quivered. David didn't understand why, but he trusted the dog's instincts to follow his lead. Suddenly, two soldiers with the Polish Army emblem on their sleeves walked by. "Boy, go home and play there!" one roared at him. David did not move. He was transfixed by their uniforms and caps, their tough expressions tempered by a note of fear in their eyes. He didn't understand why he shouldn't play in the woods and so he played on. When he returned home, he told his father what had happened. Yaakov looked at the shepherd and repeatedly murmured, "Good dog, Rex. Good dog."

To part from Rex meant the end of the world to David. Almost as hard as parting from his mother. And to lose them both was too much for him. David, too young to care what anyone thought, threw himself to the floor in grief and wept, his body racked with sobs.

When he calmed a little, he sat up and whispered, "Mom, will you take care of him? Will you put a bit of your soup on his food?"

Rivka looked at him with love and nodded her confirmation.

"And don't forget to bring him a bone from the butcher," he added. "That's how he brushes his teeth, and it's really important to brush your teeth." David quoted one of his mother's key phrases, repeated daily as she got him ready for school.

Rivka had to look away. David must never know that she could not keep Rex with her.

Chapter 3

She accompanied her family to the port, unwilling to let them go. Hugging her three children, a circle of hands, crying, breathing, laughing, and crying again. Rivka looked into her children's eyes in turn — blue, brown, and blue again. As land and sea, they anchored her. At that instant, she felt like a ship, buoyed on the waves under a cloudy sky.

She wrapped Rakhel in a big hug. "Take care of your father, your brothers. They don't know how to cook for themselves." Rivka paused and stroked her daughter's long hair. She tried, with a deep and direct look, to demonstrate and infuse her daughter with all the care, love, and knowledge Rakhel would need as the new little mother of the family.

And then there was her husband. The whole way from Warsaw to Gdansk Harbor they had been silent. Despite the tension between them, at their final parting she grew deeply emotional and hugged Yaakov to her warmly.

Finally, the blasting horn of the ship brought the send-off to an end, and she reluctantly tore herself from them.

Waving goodbye with a handkerchief, Rivka watched the ship steaming away for a long while. She still had a considerable journey back to Warsaw. Slowly, she made her way to the train station, where she stood on the platform staring into the distance but seeing nothing. The birds sang and chirped more than usual she thought. *How free they are.* The train rumbled its way to the platform and came to a shrieking, shuddering stop.

Rivka sat in a window seat, her gaze focused on the passing scenery, not looking at the commuters surrounding her. She wrapped herself in her coat, trying to recreate the warmth of her children's embraces. The pain of longing spread uncontrollably with every breath.

During the long trip, with her eyes dancing back and forth over the passing trees, Rivka felt suspended in time: She had no concerns, no worries. The constant vibration of her body to the rhythm of the rattling train slowly calmed her, and her mind emptied. She stared out the window and felt the tension and anxiety of the past few weeks finally easing. She still managed to calculate that Warsaw was the final station, so there was no possibility she'd miss it if she fell asleep. And in no time at all, her eyes closed and she sank into an uneasy sleep.

The dream ended and she awoke with drool collected on her cheek and a stiff neck. She straightened her clothes, wiped her mouth, and waited for the train to come to a complete stop. She was in no hurry, so while many passengers flew towards the exit doors, she waited patiently in her seat. There was nowhere to rush to; Rex was the only one waiting for her at home.

The front door creaked slightly when she opened it. Yaakov had neglected the house and the garden once he had decided to go, and she'd felt she was in no position to argue about it. The plates were on the table from their last meal together. She began picking up the dishes, still with leftovers on them. She whistled for Rex, and he accepted them with greedy love and licked her leg in thanks.

The German shepherd was pleasant company. Now that the house was empty, Rex was the only family left. She stroked him peacefully, looking into his brown eyes and listening to his heavy breaths. She put her thoughts away till the next day.

***

Rivka's role in the underground was to gather intelligence from operatives from all over Europe. Some messengers came to provide information, others — from Palestine — to receive encrypted data. Rex barked lustily, and due to his excessive energy, he barked at every unknown noise he heard or thought he heard. If the neighbors noticed suspicious activity, it might cost her her life and also endanger the operatives. Rivka knew she had no choice but to give Rex away.

The next morning, using a leash made from a rope she found in the kitchen, Rivka walked Rex to the home of David's friend Laser. Laser was happy to see them, and Rex jumped on him with abandon. David and Laser used to play with Rex and taught him how to fetch in Laser's backyard. Rex was familiar with the apartment and instantly made himself at home. When Rivka felt able, she thanked Laser's parents, scratched the shepherd under the chin, and asked the child to take good care of him. She closed the door behind her with a sigh. Rex must have understood that he was being left behind, and he cried out in a whimper that gave her chills. But she had no choice. She forced herself to keep going towards home.

Chapter 4

Rivka sat at their kitchen table, leaning on her fist and pulling her skin taut, making her nose look wide. One eye squinted, while the other looked down like a long-eared pup that had been left behind.

Winter was well underway, bringing with it strong winds. The ancient tree outside the house had been neglected and not trimmed this year as it had always been before. Rivka could hear the branches hitting the window with every wild gust. A loud knock at the door startled her out of her seat. She looked around warily, and anyone watching would have seen her cheek bore a deep crease from her fisted hand. At first she thought it was the tree tapping on the window as if asking to be let into the house, but when the rapping continued in a steady pattern, she realized that someone was knocking at the door.

She listened to the rhythm, trying to calm her heart so she could concentrate. It was the agreed knock, a sign that the messenger from Palestine had arrived. The messengers changed frequently, and she never knew who would be at the door. The passwords served as the security check she needed.

Rivka opened the door. The light coming in around the shadowy figure of the agent blinded her slightly. Her pupils contracted reflexively. She scrutinized her visitor briefly before inviting him in. His silhouette was wide and projected confidence and strength. When he stepped inside, she could see his green eyes held gentleness mixed with fatigue from his journey.

Rivka watched him carefully as they exchanged passwords. When she was satisfied, she pointed towards the kitchen and asked him to join her at the table.

"After all these passwords, may I now ask for your name?" she said with a smile and turned to the stove to brew a pot of tea.

When she returned with the tea, lemon, and sugar cubes in one hand, and a homemade pastry in the other, he looked at her gratefully and said, "I'm Menachem. And you?"

"My name is Rivka." She sat beside him at the head of the table and poured from the kettle. They both sat and drank.

"You're doing holy work," he said. "You know, my father and my mother moved a few years ago to Palestine. You've heard of the conflict at the Kotel — the western wall?" Menachem sipped the tea and continued without waiting for her answer. "It happened in 1929. The Arabs, in the name of Islam, fought about the Kotel with the Jews in Jerusalem. And the Jews in Morocco, from that instant, became part of the

Jews of the world. Suddenly, without another thing happening in Morocco, they were set apart."

"No, I had not heard. I'm glad you told me. And how did it happen?" she asked, watching his lips while he spoke.

"They posted propaganda in the press against the Jews, and at the same time the Jewish press was censored. People boycotted Jewish businesses. They organized prayers and fasts in support of the Arabs of Palestine and against the Zionist movement that was 'threatening' the Islamic holy places. This fray vomited my parents out, and they chose to fulfill their Zionism and went to Israel." Menachem took a long drink of tea, and Rivka's silent inquiring eyes encouraged him to continue. "I was seventeen when we went to Israel. Ever since, I've known that I must fight against the Jew-haters."

Rivka quickly did the math and determined that the handsome man sitting in front of her was about twenty-seven years old.

Menachem told Rivka his life story. "My sister, Georgette, and I were sent to a kibbutz by the Youth Aliyah. There we met new immigrants like ourselves, and for the first few months we lived in tents. Our parents were sent to a transit camp. My father worked in road construction for many hours in the blazing sun. He felt he was realizing the Zionist dream, and so he did not complain about the conditions but did the hard work with love. My mother stayed in the camp, looking for any scrap of fabric or wool to knit clothes for her children, and to sell to other families.

"The integration in the kibbutz wasn't easy. Children would tease me and my sister about our clothes and our foreign names. Giora, the kibbutz secretary, asked two young men to 'adopt' us. We were lucky because they were *tzabarim* — natives — and very nice. The one raised on the kibbutz was named Yoram, and the second, Joseph, had joined the kibbutz shortly before we arrived. My sister wouldn't leave me be and joined the three of us in all our mischief. In the evenings we built campfires, roasting potatoes as the fire died down and singing songs to our hearts' content. Yoram suggested we change our names to be more like the other children. My birth name was Prosper, which means success. I changed it to Menachem. Georgette changed her name to Leah. I was happy that Joseph liked my sister and treated her as his own.

"We made a great effort to learn Hebrew, and we willingly performed any job we were assigned to. Each evening a notice was posted on the bulletin board at the entrance to the mess hall. All the kibbutz members, including the young ones, searched for their names to see where they were assigned for the next day. In the morning we'd march off to work, and we never complained no matter how hard it was.

"Us missing our parents, brought me and my sister closer together. I was her rock and anchor due to all the changes in our lives. Every two weeks we received a weekend vacation to visit our parents. The excitement of being together was great, but it always turned into sadness when we had to say goodbye and return to the kibbutz. "

"Can I fill your glass?" Rivka suggested, rising from her seat. Her compassion for the young man came through in her soft voice.

"No, no, and thank you for listening. It's been a long time since I talked to someone like this." Rivka settled back into her chair, and Menachem continued.

"As the months passed, we started getting used to our new life and we were very happy. The youth group and the kibbutz children loved us, and Hebrew became our second mother tongue. Unfortunately, soon things changed for the worse. One evening Giora summoned us to his home. He had a long face, and I immediately sensed that something terrible had happened. After some minutes of silence, Giora hugged us and told us that a plague had spread in the transit camp. Some of the immigrants had died, including our parents.

"The shock was so great, my sister fell into my arms trembling with a heartbreaking cry. I admit, I joined her."

"I do not see shame in a man crying; it's an honest response," consoled Rivka while brushing her hair from her forehead.

"Giora sat with us for a few hours, trying to comfort us and promising to help us however he could.

"I knew right away I had to be father and mother to Leah so that she wouldn't fall apart. Yoram and Joseph stood beside us. It helped us to continue functioning.

"I consoled my sister and reminded her that the Zionist vision of our parents had left us a commitment to fulfill on their behalf. We volunteered for every kibbutz committee we could find, and we took part in every community activity. It helped us to forget and to embrace something greater than ourselves. I was left with my father's legacy to work against the Jew-haters.

"One evening Giora called me and Yoram and invited us to join a mission in Europe. At first I hesitated. Joseph encouraged me to take on the task and promised to take care of Leah. I agreed only after Leah insisted she felt strong enough. My sister encouraged me as well, and that is why you see me here. My friend Yoram is also roaming in Europe and we meet up occasionally." Menachem went quiet suddenly. He feared that he might have bothered her with the story. Who was he anyway to occupy her with the tale of his parents' deaths? Didn't she have her own problems?

Rivka told him about her family, her children and her parents. She felt comfortable sharing her secrets with him, unloading her burdens on a stranger's attentive ears. The conversation flowed easily between them, and she felt a glimmer of life and a slight blush creeping into her cheeks. The next time she glanced out the window, she was surprised to see that night had fallen.

"Do you have lodging arrangements for the night?" she asked. "You traveled such a long way!" Before he could answer, she waved her hand. "What am I even talking about? Stay here; there are enough empty rooms in this house. I will make the bed in my daughter's room. Tomorrow morning you'll get the material, but not before you eat a hearty breakfast for the road."

Menachem didn't even try to protest. He was so very tired, and the generous offer of his hostess appealed to him. He entered the bedroom on aching feet, put his bag down, and looked around at the signs of a teenage girl. A vanity table, empty of beauty products and a large mirror beside it. A carved wooden chair upholstered in a jacquard weave, and lightweight blue curtains. He tucked himself under the thick wool blanket that Rivka brought him. Her presence was evident throughout the house — the touch of her hand and her refined taste. Relaxed at last, he allowed the fatigue to take over, and he closed his eyes, letting go of the journey's difficulties.

The next morning, he woke up, washed his face, and looked deeply into his own eyes in the mirror. He ran his hand through his hair and walked into the kitchen. There was a sealed envelope waiting for him on the heavy table. This was the secret material Rivka had worked on for many months. Next to it, a steaming bowl of oatmeal garnished with fresh fruit, a slice of cake, and a cup of tea were waiting.

Rivka emerged from her room and they sat together eating and drinking. To share breakfast with company was a refreshing change for Rivka, whose days had passed in solitude since her family left. She felt a strange sensation when she waved goodbye to Menachem.

Chapter 5

After Menachem had gone, Rivka left for her job in the public library. For no apparent reason she had difficulty summoning the energy for work, even though her routine was just like the day before. She remembered enjoying the smell of the old books, the dim corridors, and the crowded bookshelves. The scattered antique tables and green lampshades illuminating the readers' books. All at once, she felt it hard to breathe, and the dust from the books was heavy on her. Rivka looked up at the high window and felt as if she were imprisoned. The belt she wore around her waist, emphasizing her hips, pressed in on her suddenly and she desperately needed some fresh air.

At the end of the workday she couldn't wait to get outside and, despite the cold, to inhale deeply. Rivka ventured through the crowds, without standing out or drawing attention to herself. She dissolved into her surroundings with her brown clothes and her drab skirt that covered her legs nearly to the ankle.

Every few days, she traveled to a clandestine meeting with

anonymous people, who gave her money for secret materials and weapons. After her husband left with the kids for America, the meetings would take place at her house. She encrypted the material she received into crossword puzzles that for the unknowing seemed innocent, like a fun game designed for children. She then put them in her son's toy chest.

She visited her parents as part of her routine, bringing a loaf of rye bread and pickled herring— deals that she found at the market. She hurried inside, bringing a breath of chilliness with her. She opened the curtains, aired the home, honored the floor with a broom, and looked around the house where she grew up.

Her mother sat in silence at the table across from her. Her blue eyes were slowly being lost to a thin film that obscured her vision, as if her eyes were no longer needed because her loved ones were gone. She brought up visions of her grandchildren that played behind her closed eyes. These images fed her aching soul. Rivka tried to put a smile on her mother's mouth, and her mother cooperated with this empty playacting. The real audience, the objects of their tender love, wasn't there and so the good cheer had faded little by little. Still, Rivka's visits brought some color to her parents' cheeks.

***

Once every few weeks, the agreed knock was heard at her door. She never knew who from among the activists would show up, but vaguely hoped each time that it would be Menachem again. They were always tired from their journey, hungry, and in need of a good shower. They found refuge in her home to rest and refresh, and sometimes they'd stay overnight. They received the encrypted material and left, but not before they had given her a payment to continue her operations. This money was used to bribe collaborators with whom she was linked.

Whenever there was a knock on her door, Rivka had a vague hope that she would see Menachem again. Whether she walked the streets or stayed at home, her thoughts were like a radio broadcast at a high volume with an announcer who never stopped, not even at night. She lay lonely and depressed in her bed. Staring at the walls, in her mind she spoke to her children. Occasionally, she spoke out loud, bringing her back to the desolate reality of her empty house. Each night when her head touched the pillow, she entered a battle she seldom won: Sleep rarely came to her. She tried to chase her thoughts away, but they only increased in the silent darkness. Sometimes she watched the lights that flickered through the curtains dancing in the breeze.

The imaginary conversations with her children persuaded Rivka that perhaps she had lost her mind. She felt her brain heating up from the incessant use. She cringed from her children's accusations carried over the ocean waves. She sensed them in the distance, calling her to help them, but she could not answer. Her tongue was stuck to her palate. Their words were daggers, and she awoke gasping in pain. And she did not know she had fallen asleep.

Rivka tossed and turned in her bed, as if she could alter the direction from which the thoughts came or change the radio station, tune in to another broadcast that would make it easier for her. Fear gripped her like a big block of ice, spreading from her stomach outwards. She could see Rakhel and tried to run to her, hold her, but her legs refused to budge. Helplessness. As her blood froze in her veins, her body no longer obeyed the commands of her mind.

The days passed, and Rivka's condition grew unbearable. The longing for her children and husband was driving her mad along with the fear that something had happened to them along the way and they never arrived at their destination. "Just let them arrive in America safe and sound," she prayed in the dark.

The first rays of morning light signaled her to get out of bed, to save herself from the folly of night. Her body was stiff and weak. Her bones creaked and cracked. Rivka slowly, painfully bent at the waist to release the pressure collected in her lower back. She hung her head down to encourage the movement of blood through the arteries to her head, to her brain. *Down, down, leave poison, leave. Go away thoughts, vanish. Let me start the day.*

Chapter 6

A loud knock awoke her from bed one night. The agreed knock. Her senses cleared at once, and she hurried to put a robe on over her gown. Through the peephole she could see the messenger. Menachem. She felt the ice trapping her melt all at once.

She opened the door immediately and noticed that he was wounded. A rag was tied around his left knee over blood-stained trousers.

"What happened to you? Come in, come in, don't stand at the door."

Menachem sat at the heavy dining table. Rivka rushed to the bathroom and returned with a first aid kit. Sitting on a chair next to him, she lifted his wounded leg and rested it on her thigh. She took off his shoe, and gently raised the trouser leg to expose his knee.

"I did not want to delay the trip, so I just tied an old shirt around it," he told her.

"Tell me how this happened to you," Rivka said as she gently cleaned the wound with gauze soaked in alcohol. Menachem tried, but failed, to suppress a grimace while she did so. The wound oozed fresh blood as she daubed at the caked blood. "Did something penetrate your leg?" she asked.

"I fell in the woods while escaping from the Germans. I was afraid I might be discovered by military personnel patrolling in the area if I kept moving, so I bound the wound, and then I hid and waited a long time to be sure they were gone."

Rivka, while making sure that nothing remained deep inside, cut boldly into the flesh, cleaned it, and sewed it up with thread, using scissors as tongs. Then she wrapped the knee up. Menachem watched her, forgetting his pain.

"And now, tea," she said, leaving his leg propped up on the chair. "You'll need lots of rest."

In the small kitchen, she put the kettle on a wooden tray along with two glasses and a cake she had baked earlier. Rivka baked for her parents and the messengers, mainly to keep herself busy. When she returned with the tray and sat next to Menachem, she felt a sharp pang of longing for her children. She missed taking care of them. A competent and able woman, she instantly became fragile and useless — a marionette laid at the bottom of the toy box to rest — her limbs powerless and weak.

Her gaze met Menachem's questioning eyes, and she couldn't control the flood of tears.

Menachem hurried to comfort his benefactress as pain poured from her like blood from his wound. He did not understand what had happened to her, but he hugged Rivka warmly to his broad chest. His body's heat pulsed inside her, melting the dams holding back her tears. Her cries hardened, and she burrowed into his embrace like an abandoned child, drawing comfort from his presence. Feeling helpless, Menachem continued his embrace, stroking her head and, with his soft murmurs, soothing her soul.

She calmed slowly and pulled away from him. "The thought that my children might need me in times of difficulty and I'm not there for them, bothers me every night. I stare at the walls and the ceiling. I try changing positions. But still, sleep refuses to come. I'm exhausted from worry and lack of sleep, and I'm afraid I will collapse soon," she said, her body shaking with sobs and chills.

Menachem took her into his arms again, her scent drifting upwards. Her essence threaded through his body, giving him a pleasant sweetness inside.

This closeness to Menachem, handsome and caring, agitated her and reassured her at the same time. Rivka felt as if she were magnetized and could not break away from him.

They sat like that, holding each other for a long while until she raised her eyes to him. He kissed her, and it sparked a flame that spread through her like a wildfire in a parched field. He stood up at once, took her by the hand, and with great effort hobbled into her bedroom.

Momentary insecurities vanished with his touch. Thoughts and worries about her family were banished to the shadows.

She closed her eyes and let the tide of pleasure take over. They made love with passion and tenderness until they both gained release. Afterwards, Rivka pressed her back against him and he wrapped his arms around her. Gentle relaxation caressed her, and finally she was able to doze off.

When she opened her eyes, she was content in the warmth of Menachem's body next to hers. Something in her was set in balance. They awoke in time to watch the sun rise, wrapped in the silence of the world before the bustle of the day. The crimson of the sunrise soon faded, and a bright light penetrated the room. They dressed, backs to each other, slightly embarrassed.

They sat comfortably together and ate the breakfast that Rivka prepared. She could not take her eyes off him. But their strong attraction wasn't merely physical; they sat and chatted for hours, as if they'd known each other all their lives.

After Rivka redressed his wound, Menachem stood up, tested his leg, and determined it was time to leave. She hesitated before she passed him the encrypted material, not ready to give him up. She gave him sandwiches and drinks for the road, and he promised to return as soon as he'd completed his mission — to get ammunition and weapons to his friends in Palestine. They had virtually no inventory left.

Neither spoke of what had passed between them, but as they embraced warmly in the doorway, both were distracted by anticipation of their next meeting.

Rivka closed the door behind him and leaned against it.

She wandered through the house revisiting her so-familiar home, all the nooks and crannies, each old stain, and every cobwebbed corner. The photos, which had waited patiently for Menachem's departure, attacked her again from all directions, passing before her eyes like a movie. Only this time, added to the torments, was her husband's image of abandonment and betrayal. Fatigue, longing, and loneliness overwhelmed her. She decided that she could not pull herself together to go to work, and when evening fell she slipped into bed exhausted, but sleep would not save her from the misery.

Images of Menachem flickered in front of her eyes. The frustration she'd felt since her family had a new focus and intensity with Menachem at its center. The next day she accepted that all she could do was continue with her daily routine and dream and hope in anticipation of his next visit.

Chapter 7

Rivka woke up from a sweet dream in the morning. She didn't know how many hours she'd spent in bed. Her body, which had awakened from a long slumber and wanted more, recalled in her dream Menachem and their impassioned communion. She awoke breathing heavily and despite being awake basked in the sensations of her dream. She clung to her pillow. So, so much she wanted to hug Menachem, but he wasn't there.

The next night passed the same way. She felt Menachem's strong arms cupping her into his chest. She heard his heartbeats with her ear pressed to the pillow. It seemed to her that she was awake all night in this fashion, listening to his heart. In truth, she slipped in and out of a sleep that brought no real rest to her weary body.

Her imagination ran over their encounter again and again, and his image strolled through the house with her. These reels of film ran around in her mind almost every night and had replaced the flashes of her children and husband. In the mornings she awoke with a new kind of guilt. The shame caught her like a knife in her belly, and she got dizzy and sick to her stomach.

Helplessness mixed with fatigue accompanied her throughout her days. When she visited her parents, they couldn't help but see their daughter's plight. Masha's questioning eyes looked at Rivka in silence. Her father asked aloud what her mother wouldn't.

"Sometimes the uncertainty tortures my soul," she shared with them. "Are they healthy? Did they succeed in their difficult crossing? Are they still on the road or was there an accident that prevented them from reaching their destination?" The guilt that greeted her in the mornings and weakened her body, she did not share. "Keep them safe," she added in a silent prayer.

Chapter 8

A loud agreed knock woke Rivka from her new life routine. Since her husband and children left, she lived completely on her own. After many weeks, Menachem stood at her front door once again. As she opened the door, the house filled with light and Rivka felt she was wrapped in his halo. It seemed to her that he was even more handsome and compelling than the character she had created from memory. Excited beyond words, she rushed him inside.

For two days, closeted in her home, they lost sense of time — even of day and night. Their passion burned so intensely they could not leave the bedroom. Even their meals were eaten there. Between the sheets, he whispered words of love and while they rested he told her how he had spent the weeks since their last meeting.

"At night, you did not leave me," he said. "My work during the day kept me busy, but in bed, you accompanied me and I felt your presence always. I curled up with your memory and found myself unwilling to wake and face each day alone."

Rivka snuggled up against him and, as she had imagined so many nights, listened to his beating heart, which threatened to burst out of his chest.

"Of all the women I've known, I've never felt like I do with you. All the affairs I've had now seem superficial and unimportant. No relationship really mattered, and they all seem distant and almost emotionless. No one touched me the way you touch me," he said in a soft whisper.

Rivka stroked his hair gently and looked into his eyes deeply, diving in, and felt his words penetrate her, just as he had minutes earlier.

"The others seemed only to want impress me. But you, you understand completely the art of touch."

Rivka, in her intimate encounters with Yaakov, had explored and discovered the secrets of his body without fear. She experienced love in the safety of that supportive union. The tender way she had once touched her husband, was now shared with her new lover

She stroked the inside of Menachem's forearm with the cushions of her fingers. She traveled up and down his body and left no part unexplored, as if she were playing the strings of his body.

"I feel like I'm on a journey, uncovering mysteries of my own body. You open my eyes, showing me so many new things. With each passing night, the mere thought of you brought back the passion and my body ached for your touch and presence." Menachem buried his nose in her neck, inhaling her scent deeply, as if he could preserve it for the road ahead.

Rivka indulged Menachem by fixing them fancy meals made with groceries she saved for him. She made the best aspic chicken in the region; however, she was unable to persuade him to eat that particular dish. Seeing the coined carrots vibrating on the jellied soup, he apologized and said that in Morocco there weren't foods like that, and the carrots were instead sweet and sugary. In particular, he was accustomed to spicy foods.

"Is it spicy you fancy?" Rivka teased and fixed him some rice-stuffed squash and peppers in spicy tomato sauce that made his ears burn. He shared his love for her with her cooking.

On the third day, early in the morning, Menachem recovered and prepared to set sail. The separation was difficult. Rivka cried in his arms. However, they both understood that they needed to return to reality. As he packed his bag, she clung to him from behind and threw her arms around him like a child. But Menachem had obligations and could not allow his feelings for her to delay or deter him.

They promised one another they would soon meet again. But fate had other plans.

Chapter 9

Menachem left Rivka's home smiling and whistling a soft tune. He made his way to the meeting place for his rendezvous with his friend Yoram. As he got close, the tune suddenly froze on his lips. Only his breath billowing in the icy air continued to testify that he was still breathing. His sharp senses told him that something was not quite right. Two men in dark clothes and hooded caps walked back and forth in front of the elderly Christian lady's shop. She often entertained him with a cup of coffee while he waited for a sign from Yoram. Without looking away, he made sharp turn behind a dense bush that hid him from the eyes of the watchers.

Hours passed, his mouth grew dry, and rumbling came from his stomach, but he did not sway from his focus. He feared an ambush and didn't come out of his hiding place. As time dragged on, the pounding of his heart slowed, but his senses remained sharp as a hunted animal's. He felt that he could hear the faintest of sounds, see the slightest of motions, and even sense the intent to move.

The insects nearby grew accustomed to his unmoving presence and began to climb over him. He was able to remain practically immobile, resisting the urge to flee. Perspiration beaded on his temples and immediately froze. Night fell and with it a light snow. He stayed vigilant and moved frugally, only enough to create a bit of warmth in his muscles. Finally, at dawn, when he felt it was safe, and his would-be ambushers had given up, he came out of hiding and approached the store cautiously.

Yoram was not there. Menachem searched for any sign that his friend had made it to the meet. Yoram liked to drink strong black coffee accompanied by a stinky cigarette, just as he had in Palestine. There was no butt in the ashtray and no cup of coffee on the old woman's table.

Menachem's stomach tightened. He decided, despite his fears, to go up to the apartment they rented from the shop owner. It was used as a meeting place and a safe refuge. He climbed the rickety stairway, moving gently on the wooden stairs and taking care to dodge the steps he knew would creak.

Darkness reigned on the landing. He did not turn on the light. The apartment door was ajar, and in the flickering moonlight he saw the remains of a struggle. Furniture, books, and papers were scattered across the floor. Menachem entered warily and opened the bathroom door. To his horror, he saw his friend lying lifeless on the tiles, his body mutilated, his neck broken, his face torn and swollen, and his skull shattered. Menachem vomited when he saw a gray, pasty liquid oozing out of a crack above Yoram's left ear. Anger and fear combined as he thought about Yoram's last moments, and he filled with renewed hatred for the Nazi agents who had slaughtered his friend.

He closed his eyes and whispered the *kaddish*. His heart was racing, and he had to decide what to do with the body. He was afraid that somebody was still on the lookout, and he knew he had to act quickly. Despite what his heart urged him, to wrap the body and take it with him, he knew that he must leave it behind. Yoram would not be honored at a funeral or receive a proper burial in the ground next to his relatives and loved ones.

Menachem quickly but carefully searched the rooms. He did not know what he was looking for, but he hoped to find some direction or a sign to show him what to do next. He tried to keep everything in its place, so as not to leave any sign of his visit. He felt grave danger in every square inch of the apartment.

He found a heavy overcoat close to his size in the closet. He decided to wear it so he'd look different upon leaving the apartment. Not finding anything important, and beginning to get desperate, Menachem was struck by a brilliant idea. Socks. That was the classic place he hid encrypted data. Indeed, Yoram's socks, which remained clean of blood, contained the treasure he'd searched for: a torn-out Polish crossword puzzle that contained the necessary information. There were marked letters revealing the hiding places of weapons purchased and ready for shipment to Palestine.

With a heavy and pain-filled heart, he left the place hoping to send others to retrieve Yoram's body and restore his honor.

Chapter 10

Menachem, crushed, walked away from the old woman's apartment. When he reached a safe place, he ripped a small tear in his shirt in the traditional Jewish sign of mourning, then he picked up a dry clod of dirt and placed it on his head. He let the dirt particles flow down his face. The grit in his eyes caused him to shut them. At once, the gruesome sight of Yoram's body flashed in the darkness, and his face contorted. He could not afford to cry or his lashes would freeze, so he stifled his grief as best he could. He could hardly breathe for the giant hand he felt gripping his throat. His distress over abandoning his best friend would not subside.

Yoram was there for him when the other children at the kibbutz had laughed at him and his sister. He'd explained to them that Prosper meant "success." Prosper-Menachem had been grateful that there was at least one righteous child among the children. Even so, he and his sister chose to change their names rather than continuing to give the kibbutz children a reason to laugh at them.

When Menachem decided to join the Zionist intelligence agency, Yoram had expressed a similar desire, and Menachem encouraged him, infecting him with a sense of purpose. He'd felt great responsibility for Yoram ever since. The decision to visit Yoram's family next time he was in Israel brought some relief from the pain. It was the least he could do.

Menachem opened his eyes, and knew that he faced another big task. If he meant to celebrate the memory of his friend, he could do so best by delivering the information Yoram had died protecting. The pressing reality did not allow him time to mourn his friend or take care of his body. The completion of the mission, the delivery of the information about the location of the weapons caches, took a few more weeks. When Menachem returned to Palestine, he finally found the courage and, despite his misgivings, he went to visit Yoram's family.

After waiting for a long while outside, he took a deep breath and knocked on the door. Yoram's father came to the door, and as soon as he saw Menachem he knew that he was about to receive bad news. He felt a weakness in his knees and his head dropped to his chest. He nodded to Menachem. Menachem didn't say a word, but his gaze delivered the message, and he confirmed it with a nod. Yoram's mother came to the door, and as soon as she realized what news had just been delivered, was overcome by weakness and fainted. Her husband picked her up, and one last look in Menachem's eyes unleashed a bitter cry.

Yoram's sister heard the scream and rushed into the living

room. She saw her father consoling her trembling mother and understood that her brother was gone. Sorrow weakened her knees as well, and she stumbled. Menachem rushed to support her, and that comforted her a little. He set her down gently on the sofa and guided her parents to seats as well. Once they were comfortable, he went to the kitchen and fetched a pitcher of ice water to help settle their nerves.

"I cannot express my grief over his death," Menachem said when he returned from the kitchen. "Yoram, your son, played an important role in vital missions for Palestine. Sacred almost."

Their sobs and wails flooded him again with his own grief and the horrors he had seen; he was determined to spare them the details of what he saw in that apartment.

"Before he died, your son helped tens of thousands of Jews get closer to the Promised Land, to freedom. Think of the Jewish state to be established thanks to Yoram and others like him, risking their lives for the sake of this sacred goal. We are hunted all over the world because of our religion and our customs, and the freedom this new country will give us to express who we are, is priceless."

They sat there for a long while, veiled with grief, sorrow, and tears. Yoram's father soothing his mother and Menachem consoling Dahlia, the little sister now deprived of a brother. Menachem used to comfort his sister, Leah, in times of crisis, and he now bestowed his warmth on Dahlia, like she was his sister.

Dahlia was grateful for his presence. Menachem's compassion enveloped her and she felt it hard to break away from his touch. Her feelings were scattered: Suddenly she was an only child, and there was something more laced in her sorrow, a kind of guilty relief. She had always felt disregarded, pushed aside because of the space taken up by her brother. And there had always been genuine unhappiness about her place in the family, because she loved her brother dearly.

And now, there was Menachem, someone she could throw all these mixed emotions at, and he responded with warmth and soothed her with his calm. Menachem had always been an object of adoration for her. All through her childhood she had tried to be a part of her older brother's group, but they rejected her and saw her as a baby. Suddenly, it seemed to her that he could solve all her problems. She prayed that the moment would last, and perhaps Menachem might feel what she felt. She studied him through a curtain of tears, out of the corner of her eye, but he gave no sign in return. Dahlia had no way of knowing that his thoughts were with another female also grieving over a brother.

Yoram's parents sat stunned. Countless questions without answers hovered around them. They refused to be comforted. Menachem made a decision to visit them whenever he could. He felt it was his moral duty, and he promised to do so.

The news spread throughout the kibbutz, and members soon began to gather at the home of the bereaved family. Most of them visited in silence, while others shared stories about Yoram's childhood and talked about his many talents. He was the first of the kibbutz to lose his life on a mission outside Israel, and sadness touched each and every one of the mourners. Most of them had no understanding of the details of his activities, they knew only that he was sent on a mission for the sake of the homeland.

Arrangements had been made for his coffin to be transported to Jaffa Port. The family had gone through terrible days waiting for it. Giora, as kibbutz chairman, had organized a delegation to go to the port in one of the kibbutz's trucks. The coffin was covered in black cloth when it was brought down carefully from the ship at dawn. They made their way back in silence, broken only occasionally by a gentle sob.

At the kibbutz gate, a tractor was waiting to take on a new job: silently carrying Yoram's coffin along the field, to eternal peace. The members carefully washed off the mud and dirt to prepare it for this somber duty. A black platform covered with flowers was hitched to it and carried the coffin on its journey around the kibbutz, and to his parents' home. Starting early in the morning, anonymous people from the security service came to pay Yoram their last respects. Menachem introduced them to Yoram's parents and his sister.

Dahlia, Yoram's sister, began reading the eulogy she had prepared but could not overcome the suffocation in her throat. The tears that overwhelmed her brought forth more sobbing from the audience, and she could not continue. Menachem hugged her and supported her until she could return to the podium, but she could read no more. He read the rest of her eulogy for her, adding his own memories and experiences.

"I will forever remember my helplessness in Yoram's last moments. The conditions and dangers of the situation prevented me from rescuing, but I swore to protect his honor and make sure he had decent burial in his homeland. I am committed to his family for as long as I live — to support them, to grieve with them, and to continue, with them, to live without Yoram. May he rest in peace.

PART TWO: YAAKOV

Chapter 11

The journey at the bottom of the ship was unbearable. A thousand or more people were crammed in there pushing each other around constantly trying to find space. A dozen languages created an unintelligible din. Among the crowd was a group of Jewish emigrants from various countries that the activists in Europe had been able to bring together and bring to the port for the big trip. Some were redeemed with money, and others escaped and hid until the moment came when they could join the journey.

Yaakov placed a bucket beside their bunk that served as a chamber pot and a receptacle for seemingly endless vomit. Each family or traveler had such a bucket that was emptied daily by tossing it over the side into the endless ocean. The buckets often overflowed and frequently spilled due to motions of the ship. The unsanitary conditions increased the level of disease on the ship without mercy. The steerage passengers with paid tickets were rarely allowed to go out on deck, and the stowaways never went above decks for fear of discovery. The air was foul with the odors of sickness, un-washed bodies, and human waste. The passengers continued vomiting even when there was nothing in their stomachs to emit. Fights broke out regularly among the passengers over a slice of bread or a favorable spot next to the single porthole, where they could lay their head.

They were cramped, overcrowded, and starving. The hunger and thirst drove them insane. The stench was suffocating. Every day, new babies were born, and every day more people died. There was no choice but to toss the bodies into the sea. The furious ocean swallowed the bodies like a hungry monster. Mothers screamed in anguish at the sight of their sons being thrown overboard.

Yaakov looked through the round window over the horizon and tried to breathe. His breath rose like clouds of memory. Day after day on the ship, he had almost forgotten what it felt like to stand on land. His life with Rivka in Poland seemed so far away. He could only focus on the present difficulties. Little David had come down with a high fever and Yaakov, Laibel, and Rakhel cared for him anxiously.

Yaakov tore a shirt into strips and found a small bowl filled with seawater. He soaked the cloth strips in the water and placed them one by one on David's forehead. Lost in his high fever, David muttered, and sometimes screamed or spoke aloud: "Mom! Come! Mom! I am a good boy, see? ... I wash my hands after the meal ..." Yaakov saw David rubbing his hands. And then: "I'm just going to take Rex out for a little while, I'll be right back, Mom ... Mom I fell ... I need a kiss ..." Yaakov saw David offer his hand, and a moment later: "It's okay now!"

Each cry was a stab in Yaakov's heart. He had a feeling that his wife's stubbornness would cause a final break between them. His heart ached for his children, who needed her now more than ever.

He adjusted the cloth on David's forehead. He had no other means of helping him. For many days he sat beside David's bed and feared for his life. From time to time his son opened his eyes. A glimpse of hope soared in Yaakov's heart. In those moments, Yaakov talked to him. "David, David, can you hear your father? David, you hear me, you're going to get better. All you have to do is say, 'I'm healthy!' Expel the illness; tell it you don't want it in your body."

When David seemed to understand his words, Yaakov continued. "You need to be healthy and strong, someday you'll see your mother again, when this journey is over. You do want to see your mother, right?" David struggled and nodded. After many more days, the little boy grew stronger and finally he recovered.

Yaakov and his children held on to life itself. That was why he had left. It was hard for him to travel to the unknown, breaking up a warm family unit, everything he had built. Yaakov had spent many good years with his wife at his side. He had diligently set aside money in those years of abundance. Those savings had been useful, as he'd had to bribe officials to get their papers during the immigration process.

He'd read the map correctly and had seen the skies darkening over his country's Jews and over all the Jews of Europe. He knew he had to save his children, the source of his strength. He did not understand how Rivka could abandon their children, and deep anger bubbled again in his heart. But he didn't have much time to concentrate on his anger. The next pitch of the ship sent him quickly to his bucket, and he vomited again.

Some people turned out to be leaders, and they worked to calm people's spirits. They tried to keep the children busy and distract them, but few were willing to cooperate. Someone came to Yaakov's children as well, but that only helped for a short time.

Yaakov brought David up to the deck after he recovered. It was important to him that David breathe some germ-free, fresh air. "Grab my shoulders. You're still too weak." In truth, Yaakov needed some fresh air as well.

"Okay, Dad," David replied.

They were at sea, and the crew wasn't as strict about keeping them inside the ship. Yaakov climbed up the rickety metal stairs, one step at a time, and waited for David to follow. His son stopped at every step, took a deep breath, and reached for the next step. Finally on the open deck, Yaakov supported David, who had wrapped his arms around his father's shoulders. They stood quietly, listening to the seagulls' cries, and reveling in the fresh air. The sun and the salty breeze returned the color to David's cheeks. Yaakov could breathe deeply as well. There is no way to describe Yaakov's relief that David was out of danger.

Suddenly, a thought came to Yaakov. He realized that if there were seagulls, it was a sign that they were approaching land! He squinted his eyes. Through the mist he could see the lady of liberty approaching, and Ellis Island's tall Ferris wheel.

Yaakov's elation flooded him from head to toe. "It's over!" he called. "This nightmare is over." He began humming softly, as happy as could be, and a faint smile of relief brightened up David's face as well. "We have arrived, my son, do you understand? We have arrived at last!" David's smile widened. He realized that he was saved, and this time for good.

The ship finally docked at Ellis Island. They still had to wait many long hours for authorization to unload them to shore. When they got off the ship, they joined the long lines of weak and starving people. Yaakov touched the immigration certificates he had purchased for a lot of money. He'd kept them from harm, close to his body, and even so they had become frayed over the weeks. His whole life was bound to those pieces of paper.

His new life. His family's life. He was so eager to start it, but when they finally felt solid ground under their feet, they learned that Ellis Island was but a large camp set up by the American authorities to classify the refugees from burning Europe. Every immigrant had to undergo rigorous medical testing. The authorities wanted to prevent the introduction of incurable diseases to the continent. David was detained for further investigation because he did not seem quite well. But they determined that his illness was behind him and gave him permission to move along.

After the examinations, Yaakov and his children moved into a large hall and settled in a corner. Some immigrants had been barred from entering, and their fate was unknown. Yaakov and his children slept on mattresses, huddled together for comfort. The living conditions of the makeshift encampment at Ellis Island dampened Yaakov's spirit, but he encouraged himself by remembering that it would be over soon. Very soon. All his hopes and prayers were directed to his sister, Hannah, that she would find a way to release them soon, amen.

Chapter 12

When Hannah and Icho-Isaac settled in the Bronx, they joined immigrants like themselves and the group became like a close family with shared memories and a shared past. Icho gathered all his friends and realized not all had useful professions. One was a plumber, one a painter, two were drivers, one a builder, another a watchmaker, and there was even a shoemaker. He formed a construction company that worked on building renovations. Even if one of his friends did not have a defined profession, Icho included him and found him a job. These friends began to specialize in apartment moves, and they also packed up furniture and moved it to new addresses. First in vans and over the years in trucks Icho acquired.

Icho and Hannah became the backbone of the community. They spent the holidays at home and set up long tables at Rosh Hashanah and Passover for guests. Wine makes one cheerful and brings out secrets as well. The rejoicing was always diluted by heartache and longing for their loved ones left in Europe.

They used the Christian holidays to take trips and explore their new country, America. Hannah was a hard-working woman. Not only with regards to the social gatherings and the strengthening of the small community, she also liked putting hers to work. Her talent with a needle and a thread was used to advantage not only in repairing her family's clothes, but also to bring in some money. She sewed fancy curtains for the high society women of New York. Soon, she started getting requests for tailored dresses. The word of her talent spread, and her working hands did not rest.

Icho also did well, and the company expanded. They lived in a sort of prosperity that they hadn't had for a long time. Icho was so busy with management that he started hiring people to do some of the work he had been in charge of until then. An accountant was hired to conduct the finances, and secretaries were recruited to answer the many phone calls.

Alex, Icho's friend, along with participating in the renovation business, worked as a translator at Ellis Island. His language skills allowed him to perfect Polish, Russian, Czech, and German. In addition, he quickly learned English, making him a great asset to the United States authorities. When Hannah learned that her brother, niece, and nephews were stuck on Ellis Island she asked Alex for his help, and offered him a hefty amount to help secure their release.

Alex wandered the halls in search of Yaakov and his children, as he had promised Hannah, while Yaakov and his children wandered around the buildings trying to find something

to eat. There wasn't much food available, and they had to settle for scraps even in the land of abundance. Yaakov bit his
tongue and kept repeating the mantra that everything was
temporary and that Hannah would soon rescue them from
this cesspool.

They found a corner that had been set up as a snack area,
with supplies for passengers to prepare coffee and tea. The
family pounced on dry cookies they found and devoured
them hungrily. After that, they poured some of the sugar for
tea and coffee into their hands, and put it in their mouths.
David wetted his finger and ate the sugar little by little so
it wouldn't run out so quickly. After their stomachs settled
somewhat, Yaakov asked for his children to be able to bathe,
so Hannah wouldn't see how dirty they were. But the show-
ers were in a common area with dozens of people showering
openly together, mud was everywhere, and the terrible stench
of toilets filled the air.

Rakhel chose to remain dirty and not to strip in front of
others. David and Laibel shed their filthy clothes willingly,
even though they had no clean clothes to put on. Still, Yaakov
searched through his belongings and pulled out some shirts
that were less dirty. He poured some water on the children's
grimy bodies, and after the "cleaning ceremony" they put on
the shirts that their father offered them.

Alex was looking for a man with a daughter and two sons.
He carried pictures of the family that Yaakov had sent Hannah.
He saw a man and his two sons dressing, all were neglected

and emaciated. He was about to leave for another room when suddenly, out of the corner of his eye he saw Rakhel. Rakhel, the only one who still resembled her photograph. It was hard to miss her pale blue eyes. Her hair, though it was filthy, was carefully braided, and it was obvious that she tried to present herself well. Alex's eyes widened when he realized that this sorry group was Hannah's family.

"Yaakov?" he asked hesitantly.

The scruffy and scrawny man raised his head with questioning eyes.

"Hannah sent me to get you out of here. Come with me."

Yaakov thanked him quietly, and his face brightened with a cautious smile. "Finally," he whispered, "our misery is over."

Alex managed to arrange their release immediately after the procedures with the authorities were done. Yaakov barely hobbled along and the staggering children fell behind. In this way, with their last strength, they reached the camp gates. Hannah was waiting for them on the other side.

"*Oy, vey ist mir* ..." Hannah's lips muttered when she laid eyes on her brother. His eyes were sunken, and his body was emaciated — his clothes hung on his body as on a hanger. His children were ragged and dirty; David was the thinnest and sickliest of them all.

Hannah handed them warm, clean blankets of soft wool, and they wrapped themselves in them. They rode in silence in Icho's truck to Hannah's home in the Bronx. They watched the passing scenery of their new country in shock. The tall buildings, the lights, the hustle and bustle. So different from the pace of Europe. They almost forgot their aching bodies, so entranced by what they saw.

Eight concrete steps separated Hannah's home from the sidewalk. The family gratefully entered the beautifully decorated house, evidence of Hannah and Icho's prosperity. Inside it was nice and warm. Two streams of tears left clean trails on Yaakov's smoky face. His lips trembled. All the despair and anxiety he had suppressed during his trip, staying strong for his children, rushed up and grabbed at his throat. He rushed out to the patio, where he finally allowed himself to cry in achy and cleansing sobs. Hannah took the children by the hand and hurried to give them clean clothes then sent them to wash their bodies one by one.

When Yaakov came back in, Rakhel, Laibel, and David were cleaner and better smelling than they'd been in a long time. Then, it was his turn. Yaakov asked Icho for a clean towel and a razor. He cut his hair with some scissors and then moved on to his beard, finishing up with foam and a razor. He scrubbed his body vigorously, as if he could erase the past as easily as he shed his dead skin cells. He was preparing himself for this new world by brushing away the dirt of his previous life.

Clean and free from the past, he stepped into the living room. Rakhel had helped Hannah to set a beautiful table. It was the eve of Sabbath. At sea, every day was like every other. Occasionally, they got together a prayer quorum but he could never tell what day it was. But that was now behind them. Here, there was a big, sweet challah resting on a silver tray covered with a white napkin. The candelabras shined. White plates and silver forks on napkins graced a long table.

Icho asked Yaakov to preside over the blessing. The new immigrant blessed the food devoutly. There was much magic in that simple action. Even the children felt it. Young Laibel was in awe. He had never felt such sweetness. Everything was still inside and out. Silence.

Yaakov's prayer could be heard from afar. Holiness came down over the table and they felt united. Yaakov broke the bread, dabbed it with salt and passed it out to everyone present. Slight echoes of the "amen" brought them back to the table.

They ate in silence, and only the tapping of forks and knives on plates testified that there was movement. When the meal was over, they stayed a little longer gazing at the candles that Hannah and Rakhel had lit earlier. They were sucked into the halo, each deep in memories.

The next day, Yaakov and his sons went to the synagogue with Icho. They asked for prayer shawls from the *gabay* of the synagogue, and the rabbi's gentle smile and warm eyes welcomed them warmly. Laibel found himself praying, and for the first time he understood the essence of the prayer. His eyes closed, and he added a silent prayer for his mother's well-being.

Little David asked God to watch over his mother and his

dog. He treasured a coin that he had received as a gift from his mother and he held it close to his heart. He tried to hold on to it and to the image of his mother, and not get carried away in the stream of prayers and the synagogue's bustle.

Things were getting better.

Hannah rented an apartment for her brother about a half hour away. Six months' rent was her gift to her brother and his family in their new country. It was the least she could do for them after all their hardships.

Yaakov felt it proper for his children to receive a Jewish education and to remain within the traditions of Judaism and not to assimilate in the foreign land. The decision to enroll his sons in the yeshiva of the Jewish community was made easier by the fact that they didn't charge him anything for the boarding school.

Chapter 13

As she had no choice, Rakhel took on the role of the home-maker, a job that was hard on her. She tried to give their apartment the appearance of a real home. They could not throw out the old furniture that came with it because they couldn't afford to replace it. All she could do was to air it out, rearrange, and beautify. One thing she did change: She took down the old curtains and sewed new ones that reminded her of her mother's home using a lightweight blue tablecloth for the fabric. She scrubbed the floors and the kitchen cabinets. She evicted their current tenants carefully and instead installed a set of china that she received from her Aunt Hannah. She even polished the silver cutlery that her aunt had given them and put it in the drawers. She made their beds with clean and simple sheets, and made their modest home fit for living. The boys joined in by sweeping the leaves from the steps that led to the apartment building.

The money they'd brought with them was meager and would only last for a few weeks. Yaakov knew he had to hurry up and start earning a living, so as soon as he was able to find the right spot, he rented a small carpentry shop at the edge of Manhattan, and with his talented hands he made unique furniture.

Jacob, they called him. He offered his customers a cup of tea with lemon and a sugar cube, just like he used to drink with Shlomo. He sat with them drinking tea and planning the furniture they dreamed of. They described the layout of their homes and he advised them how to take advantage of the space and what furniture was needed.

In between the design and the furniture, he learned a bit about their lives and so became a sort of consultant on family matters. Here he planned a kitchen kingdom, over there he designed a work area that allowed concentration and privacy. His furnishings, beyond the fact that they were masterpieces, often brought peace to the home as well as beauty.

His reputation grew, and the flow of customers increased. He found himself spending more time in the shop than at home — consulting with his brother-in-law Icho's construction business, consulting with other families, while his own family was neglected. At the shop he thrived, while at home he had to handle the difficulties of caring for a family without a mother. He'd never had to deal with raising his children before. Rivka was always the one who'd listened to the needs of their souls, worried about their daily tasks from the crack of dawn till the time they went to sleep. She worried about keeping them clean, feeding them properly, reading bedtime stories as well as supplying all their emotional needs.

He did not know what to do, how to deal with all of this. Yaakov told himself that the money he brought home would compensate for his absence and the absence of their mother and thus give them a better future, so he spent twice as much effort in his work. Rakhel had to be the acting mother, and all the while she looked for a way out of that life.

Laibel and David began to study the Torah in English, which was still foreign to them. In the first weeks they felt mute and were mere spectators in the classroom. When they finally tried to speak out, heavy Polish accents accompanied their words.

Rakhel had learned basic English from her grandmother and quickly adopted the New York accent. She also made it a point that to strangers, her name from then on would be Rachel and she would be like a true American. The boys occasionally still spoke Yiddish like they did at home, but the world outside demanded English everywhere. The boys got permission to be at home every two weeks because of their family's recent arrival in the country.

Soon they learned the simple words that were required at random encounters: Hello. How are you? Thank you. You're welcome. Please. Their world narrowed to beginnings and endings. All of the middles remained silent and unspoken.

She invested all the effort she could bear to prepare the boys a good meal when they returned from long days of study. And so the three of them sat down for dinner at home:

a soft-boiled egg, some white bread dipped in the egg, a few vegetables and a spoonful of soft cheese. On Fridays she baked a cake that they ate all week and after dinner was over they awaited it impatiently.

Yaakov-Jacob came home later in the evening. He found his two sons sprawled on the couches. Rakhel was closed up in her room. No one had run to him, as if they were powerless to rise from where they lay.

"Shalom," he announced upon entering.

David and Laibel, each wrapped in his own world, did not hear him.

"Shalom," he called aloud again. This time his greeting was tinged with annoyance. "I've been working all day to support you, the least you can do is say hello to your father when he comes home."

Laibel said, "Hello and welcome."

David, still in his inner world, didn't answer.

"What about you, David!" Yaakov called angrily.

David ran to his room. *No one understands me, he thought to himself. I want my Mommy. Why isn't my mother here? Mommy! Why did you leave me?* Stinging tears rose in his throat.

Laibel walked into the room quietly and saw his brother lying on his stomach. Silent tears trickled into his pillow. "Here, read this prayer," he said, handing David an open prayer book. "You must surrender to the Creator. Read, read."

David turned his head away. Laibel set the *siddur* bedside

David's bed and left the room. After his brother walked out, David threw the book and it slammed against the wall. "Surrender to the Creator ... eh?" he muttered.

Chapter 14

Hannah invited Jacob and his children for a family dinner every Friday. Laibel loved those peaceful times. The sweetness of the Sabbath was always felt in her home despite the tumult on the streets of New York.

The Bronx was saturated with Jews. They tried to preserve their traditions and keep kosher without assimilation. Hannah started to whisper in Jacob's ear the idea of soon matching Rakhel to a good, God-fearing Jew. Jacob smiled, he was relieved that Hannah had offered to help him. Her assistance eased his job as a single father. Her children were grown, and her grandchildren, who were born in America, always laughed and played after dinner. At those times Jacob could really rest; he felt that everything had straightened out and was in line in with the intention of the Creator.

The weeks passed and Jacob partnered with his brother-in-law's company, which had greatly expanded, opening additional branches in other cities of New York. Many new employees were hired. Icho organized the company into departments by specialty and chose his best people to head up the departments. Jacob was appointed to manage the department that dealt with carpentry — the construction of kitchen cabinets and furniture. He had not forgotten the pleasure he received from crafting special furniture, and occasionally he allowed himself time to create a unique table that at the end was sold as a piece of art.

Rachel felt her father had made peace with his new situation. He stopped grumbling and left for work every morning clean-shaven and smelling of pleasant scents she wasn't familiar with in Poland. He had also stopped hounding David, although he was the only one who continued to suffer from separation anxiety and could not stop longing for his mother. Rachel attributed her father's new behavior to the satisfaction of managing a big department in her uncle Icho's company and the large amount of money he earned. Little did she know that her father had met a woman, Clara, a clerk in the office.

However, Jacob did share the secret of Clara with Hannah. Hannah was happy for him and encouraged him by saying he deserved to start a new chapter in his life. They decided not to tell Icho because they didn't know how he'd react. Those were Jacob's happiest days. They lasted a few months until near the time of Hanukkah.

Hannah, Icho, their children, and grandchildren, decided to go on a vacation. The grandchildren, sitting in the backseat of the car, were very excited. They laughed and talked loudly even after being shushed many times, and Icho, who was driving, turned around to yell at them to be quiet. He turned his attention back to the road to find an approaching truck in his lane. He quickly turned the wheel and crashed into a tree. The fuel tank exploded, and within minutes the vehicle was engulfed in flames.

Jacob was informed of all that when the authorities tracked him down as Hannah's only relative. When the officers who had brought the news left the shop, Jacob locked the door behind them. He sat back in his chair. He rubbed his knee, and suddenly it seemed to him that it was colder than ever inside. The expression on his face froze, and the number of furrows on his forehead seemed to have doubled.

When he returned home, Jacob forgot to argue with David about saying hello and simply collapsed into his favorite brown armchair. There he sat and stared at nothing at all. David glanced at his father with renewed dolefulness that Rex wasn't with him. At least then he would have the attention and the love of a real friend.

The next morning David didn't get up from his bed; he just didn't see the point. Each busy with their own business, no one noticed. In the evening Rachel went up to him wondering why he hadn't come to the table to eat dinner with them. "Are you okay?" she asked.

"Yes," he answered shortly.

Rachel withdrew. She decided to let it go and let him come when he wanted.

"Dad, why is it that Aunt Hannah didn't invite us for

Sabbath?" Rachel asked.

Jacob had to tell his children the horrible news. He called them into the living room. David came reluctantly. He was tired and weak because he refused to eat. After everyone sat down, Jacob cleared his throat before he started talking. "My dear children, you know that I decided to bring you to America to give you a better future. And also to be close to my sister Hannah and her family so they could help me with raising you.

"I must tell you the sad news of the premature deaths of Hannah and her family in a car accident. When their bodies arrive in New York, we will hold their funeral. Dear Rakhel, you help us always to the best of your ability, but I ask of you again for your help with the funeral arrangements. Go see the rabbi, and he will tell you what we are to do."

Stunned, the boys stayed seated, while their sister left the house to talk to the rabbi.

When the time came, since they had no other relatives, they sat *shiva* among themselves and only the rabbi from the yeshiva came to visit. He brought men with him for a quorum and offered his condolences.

For many days, David did not get out of bed. He could not find a reason to get up in the morning. At night he cried softly, and in the morning he found no reason to part with the world of his dreams. He felt pleasant and warm in there. There, he saw his mother. There, he played with his dog. But even there he was upset with his mother for leaving him. He was upset with his father. And he was even upset with Aunt Hannah, who found the worst time to leave him.

He had a hard time falling asleep and resting. One night he wondered to himself what it would be like to die. To go to a better world without suffering. Was his mother still alive, he wondered. It might just be easier to cross that threshold, cross that narrow bridge. To join his mother, his aunt, and his family and to see whether there was indeed a God, waiting at the gates.

One night he made a long rope from his sheet, and in the morning Rachel found him lifeless. A chilling shriek tore through the house. Laibel ran and saw his brother; his lips automatically began to murmur a prayer.

Laibel, full of tears, rushed to tell his father the terrible news. Laibel waited until the customers left, then closed the door and told his father that David was found hanging in his room, dead. Laibel was distraught and hoped his father could offer him some solace.

But instead, Jacob fell to his knees. He started screaming and throwing sawdust everywhere. Enraged, he picked up a hammer and started pounding on the unfinished creation that rested on the sawhorse. Wood chips flew all over. He slammed all the tools on the floor. Laibel found himself dodging barrages of weapons.

Finally, Jacob collapsed on the floor and began to cry, talking to himself. The frothy saliva mixed with the thin sawdust. Laibel almost did not recognize his father in this crazed state. After some time, Jacob calmed and went into a state of inertia and near-paralysis.

Laibel brought him home.

This time, they would share their grief with no one; it would not leave their home.

Chapter 15

At the end of shiva, Jacob returned to the shop. He walked in and sat down. He stared at the walls and could not bring himself to even hold a saw. All the joy he knew was lost. The carpentry shop phone on the wall rang and rang; Jacob did not answer.

***

There was a gentle knock on the heavy metal door. Again and again it repeated. Jacob did not respond; maybe he didn't even hear it. Suddenly, the door was pushed open. Clara stood at the threshold. Even though she'd only known Jacob for a short while, she felt she should come to the shop to see if he would accept her condolences.

Jacob got up and opened the door all the way. "Thank you. Thank you for coming. You didn't have to," he muttered.

Clara offered him a cup of tea and some pastry from a nearby delicatessen. He looked at her vacantly and felt distant. He shouldn't have come to America. But what was waiting for him in Europe?

"I made a mistake. I should have gone to Israel ..." he muttered.

Clara looked at him with pity. Her heart went out to him, and she just wanted to ease his pain. "It's not your fault, Jacob. You did the best you could ..." She tried to comfort him.

His whole body ached. Clara tried to hug him, but he suddenly could not bear her touch. "Do not feel sorry for me, Clara. I don't deserve it. Indeed, I am responsible, but it weighs too heavily on my shoulders. And I'm only one man. My children's lives depend on me, and I've let them down. I tore them from their mother, and for what? For more loss and mourning? David, my little boy. For many weeks I took care of him in his sickness. He overcame it! The thought that he would see his mother again kept him alive.

"We all hoped so much that our miseries would end as soon as we set our feet on the soil of the Promised Land! But they just started again. Another chapter of pain. I don't know if Rivka is alive, whether she has survived the horrors the Jews suffer in Europe. And if she will ever know that our son, the youngest, David, is dead.

"How many more losses will I have to bear? I cannot take it anymore, Clara. I don't deserve to be a father to my children. If only I had scolded him less ... why was it so important that he said hello to me when I came home? I didn't think to check what was going on with him.

"David, my son, you missed your mother so much that you wanted to see whether she was waiting for you on the other side? You were alone. You were just alone. How did we not see it? The death of Hannah and her entire family was a terrible blow. Even for me. Everyone was absorbed in themselves. I didn't see him. I did not see you ... David, my son." Jacob had trouble breathing and felt that everything was closing in on him; his tears were choking him. He did not want to fall apart in front of Clara. He needed to get out of there.

"I am so sorry. Thank you for coming to comfort me," he said in a choked voice and ran out, leaving Clara behind with her own pain.

"Jacob! The shop isn't locked," she called out weakly, but he could not hear her.

For hours, Jacob walked the streets of New York.

His eyes were flooded, and the buildings he passed were distorted through the pool of tears. He noticed things he had not seen before. A beggar sitting on the side of the road with his head bowed, his shoes untied, and his coat torn. Their eyes met for a second before Jacob moved on. He watched the steam rising from the manholes, columns of smoke from under the streets. New York's buildings seemed grayer than ever. He eventually arrived at the beach promenade, where high waves greeted him. There, he felt the wind even more.

It seemed to him that the world had slowed down. It was gloomy and dull, reflecting his mood precisely.

Jacob came to a tavern. He sat at the bar and asked for a

strong whiskey. He drank it at once. His throat burned, and then a warm feeling spread throughout his body. For a while he was able to forget his suffering.

***

During the day, Laibel was in school, and at night he joined Rachel at home. Neither could penetrate their father's grief and talk to him. Initially, Jacob continued to leave the house for work in the morning, but he couldn't find the emotional strength to actually work. Instead, he walked the streets, usually ending up in bars to ease the suffering. Only a few years before, alcohol was banned across America. Now everything was available. Bars on every corner, shops selling alcohol. The bottle had winked at him. It had called him to ease his suffering, and he had answered.

He was trapped in a vicious circle. Loitering, drinking, vagrancy. At the end of the day, he came home and collapsed on the couch.

Rachel had to care for her father. Despite her own grief, she at least knew how to function in a time of crisis. She kept him clean and prepared his meals. First, her only request was that Jacob not loiter in bars and spend money he did not earn. That, however, didn't stop him from drinking. But at least he no longer found himself in dark corners of the city. She cooked nutritious meals and made sure he drank plenty of water. Jacob was the patient, and she was the devoted nurse.

She found a job with a modest salary at the central post office. She stopped the family from going downhill to oblivion. Slowly, she asked him to reduce his alcohol intake. Jacob did as she asked.

Laibel didn't respond as well to David's death, and especially to his father's reaction. He blamed his father for everything. He was the one who had taken them away from their mother, and because of his neglect David had committed suicide. And more than that, after everything that had happened Jacob had forgotten that he was the father. His role was to take care of his children, not vice versa.

Laibel was agonized for weeks. Luckily, the rabbi had devoted a great deal of attention to him, and in response to his grief, Laibel found himself increasingly delving into his studies. At least there he knew temporary relief from his aggrieved soul.

Laibel was clinging to religion and slowly distancing himself from his father, until he preferred not to talk to him anymore. He didn't want to feel the pain, the anger that he felt towards him. Nor to open wounds that time and distance were helping to heal.

Gradually this family, that once was happy and united, became fractured. Wandering souls in the maze of life. Each lost in their own different way.

PART THREE: RIVKA

Chapter 16

Europe was invaded and conquered, with Poland falling first. Yellow patches began to appear as stars in the dark skies, giving away and identifying the Jews as targets. Rivka brushed her golden hair, looked straight into her blue eyes in the mirror and decided to pull down her jacket's collar a bit and to hide the yellow star with her scarf. She was wearing a brown suit that she had received from her Polish neighbor. She hadn't decided yet whether to go with pride and emphasize her fair skin to avoid the fate of her Jewish identity or to assimilate in the brown color of her clothes and stick to the edges of the houses and streets to attract as little attention as possible. Finally, she decided to do both. She gathered her hair like her peasant neighbors, blurred the signs of her femininity, and adopted a purposeful walk. She chose not to be afraid and walk around like a mouse, as that might be the way to be noticed.

She had to keep up with her underground activities, but as a Jew, she was forbidden to use public transportation and so she traveled considerable distances on foot. She walked forward, focused, when she went out. But mostly, Rivka tried to stay confined to her home and to leave only for intelligence gathering or to obtain food.

Two days after Warsaw's opposition against the Nazi occupiers was defeated, the Judenrat was established. The Judenrat was comprised of selected notable people of the community. Initially, the people rejoiced that this Jewish council would act as their representative with the Germans. At that point they still believed that cooperation would save them.

The Judenrat undertook a census. Names, addresses, ages, and professions. All the properties of Warsaw's Jews were mapped. The Jews were forced to mark not only themselves but also their businesses.

The Nazis started to send men from the age of fourteen to forced labor. Rivka had chills down her spine when she thought of Laibel and Yaakov. She and her parents had earned only a little more time. How happy she was about Yaakov's determination about leaving. The invaders had begun looting and confiscating property. Rivka looked around her home; nothing of value was left for them to take. Their savings had been needed by Yaakov for the trip to America and to establish a life in the new country.

She finished all her tasks by afternoon, so she could be at home by sundown in time for the nighttime curfew. The streets were deserted except for some guards patrolling. Like a fast and insidious crawling creature, the decrees crept up one by one. Within weeks, the order was given to move the Jews to a living area designated for Jews only, with the false claim that this was precaution against typhus. What choice did they have?

They hadn't reached her town of Nadvorna. However, the Judenrat in Warsaw completed the transition to the ghetto in three days. The ghetto was separated from the rest of life in Warsaw by a high wall. The Nazis confined an area of about ten blocks. They moved a hundred thousand Polish people out and moved a hundred and eighty thousand Jews in. The severe overcrowding and the poor sanitation increased disease and mortality.

The Judenrat tried to make life in the ghetto easier. They developed institutions that served the Jews and created an attitude of mutual aid in times of need. Classrooms, soup kitchens, and charities were opened along with businesses. At first, they were able to go beyond the walls, but later they risked their lives in doing so. Those who managed to smuggle lived like kings, especially compared to the hungry children with their stretched bellies. The rich lived in a small section of the ghetto and only a narrow pedestrian bridge connected them to the bigger part, where most lived in buildings half-destroyed by fires and bombs.

More and more Jews were confined to the ghetto, and the severe overcrowding grew even worse. Thin, starving children often tried to escape to the other side of Warsaw and bring a little food back inside. It was a dangerous undertaking, but they had nothing to lose. Bodies were stacked in the streets of the ghetto. People collapsed from exhaustion and hunger.

All this time, Rivka and her parents kept a low profile, and the information exchange had slowed down significantly. Rivka, who had managed to remain in her home in the suburbs of Warsaw, knew that she must refrain from going to the ghetto at all cost.

The boys who escaped the ghetto would come to her house once in a while, and she shared with them the little food she was able to get. A potato here. An onion there. Even these would light up their eyes. She thought of her own children. She prayed they had full stomachs and was grateful her husband had taken them away.

One morning she awoke and heard a commotion outside her house. She looked through the peephole and froze. There was a loud knock at the door, and it was immediately broken in.

"*Schnell!*" two officers barked at her and grabbed her arms.

She was taken to the town square and saw all her neighbors and her parents already there. "Mother!" she cried softly and slowly approached her parents. They each carried a suitcase with valuables that they had asked to take with them. Their neighbors walked beside them cowering and in complete silence; their eyes were wild with fear. The random cry of a child was silenced immediately by the parents. They stood a long while in the hot sun.

"You've got to find my grandchildren," Masha said. "You must live!"

Rivka's father looked deeply into her eyes without saying a word and immediately looked back down.

A platoon of German soldiers spread out, surrounding them. Rivka watched them carefully, and what she saw in their eyes made her sick to her stomach. *What I feared has come*, she thought, and right then, the soldiers opened fire. Deafening shrieks assaulted her ears. Bodies flew through the air in slow motion spraying blood as she watched in horror.

"Rivkahhhhh!" her father yelled, and then the terrifying noises and hideous screams went silent, and only the sound of gunshots was heard, thundering in her ears. She went into shock, her limbs paralyzed. She watched numbly as her neighbors fell like wheat surrendering to the sickle. One after the other like dominoes, toppling the ones next to them. Then terrible stillness.

The clatter of horseshoes on cobbles revived her from fainting to a strong nausea. Rivka's mind worked quickly. She realized that if she wanted to see her children again, she must keep from being heard. She could not move. Bodies settled into their final rest on top of her, pressing on her lungs. Her breathing was labored, and her lips murmured a silent prayer. Blood pounded in her temples, but she had to wait, struggling against the instinct to get out, to breathe.

Her senses sharpened, and it seemed that she heard everything. Darkness had begun to descend and the cold of night was coming. Still, there were no sounds of people. She came to accept that she was the only one who survived.

The bodies of her friends and neighbors were growing rank, but they kept her warm. The forced labor workers hadn't come yet to evacuate the bodies and that gave her a little more time. She moved two bodies aside carefully, and fresh air rushed into her lungs. But before she could savor the deep breath and inhale again, she realized to her horror that the bodies she had pushed aside were those of her mother and father.

Rivka kissed her mother's hand and touched her father's face. His eyes were wide open, his mouth slightly parted. Saliva and blood had collected in his beard. His last cry was still on his lips. With a choked sob she whispered a prayer for their souls. She hurried to crawl away quietly to a building at the edge of the square, fronted by columns. She hid behind one of the pillars among crates collected there. She stayed there that night, determined to do whatever it took to see her children again.

In the morning she watched the workers clearing the bodies from the square. Again, revulsion came over her, and she vomited quietly. To avoid detection, she waited in her hiding place while the removal continued. The stench of urine and vomit was nearly unbearable. Hunger and thirst plagued her. Fatigue threatened to close her eyes. Her lips dried, and she tried to moisten them with her tongue. That worked briefly until her mouth dried and small cuts appeared.

On the second night she heard German voices coming from the second floor, and Rivka realized that the Nazis had established their headquarters up there. Had her luck run out? Fear temporarily incapacitated her, but then her sharp instincts recovered and she resolved to escape from there as soon as possible.

Chapter 17

For two days she huddled in the crates, trembling with fear all day and shivering with cold at night. Around sunset on the third evening, she decided it was time to go. Hunger and the thirst would soon overcome her, so she determined to get to the forest. She knew the area well. She'd heard that the partisans hiding in the woods helped terrified refugees like herself reach ships that brought them to Palestine. She understood she had no choice. She would do the only thing she could and then later look for her family in America.

She recalled that the partisan activity was concentrated at the northern edge of the forest. She had to be careful not to fall into the hands of the non-Jewish partisans. They were known to murder Jews fleeing for their lives. The Jewish partisans were very secretive. As guerrilla units, they had to rely on the Polish farmers who lived near the forests for food and a place to hide. They were not often welcomed by the farmers, and weapons were difficult to come by. Therefore, they often joined the socialist underground, or set up as independent

Jewish units. These brave men, who were accustomed mostly to city life, left their families behind to their own fate, in order to fight and save Jews from certain death.

Under the fast spreading darkness, Rivka came out of hiding. Taking her fate in her own hands she started walking. She was very weak, and progress was slow. Occasionally she stumbled over rocks and fell, continuing her journey on hands and knees until she could recover. Her determination gave her body strength she didn't know she had. She discovered droplets of water on the roadside plants where it accumulated on the inside of the leaves, next to the root. She savored it like it was the last water on earth. Her eyes closed, enjoying the sensation of moisture on her tongue. So much power in a few drops of water. She never knew that simple water could come to mean so much.

In the road ahead, she saw a uniformed figure walking towards her. It was a German officer accompanied by a leashed attack dog. Her body reacted automatically, before she even had time to think. As quietly as she could, Rivka scurried to an opening in a roadside fence and hid behind a broken gate. She held her breath in terror, trying not to even move a finger. With one eye peering through a crack, she saw the dog whining, pulling its master towards her. There was nothing she could do. Nowhere she could run without being seen, and it was clear that if she tried to run she'd be gunned down.

This cannot be happening. It cannot be that I escaped the massacre only to be caught by a dog! Rivka's outrage was real.

The dog reached her hiding spot, and Rivka was revealed. *My fears have come true*, she thought. Her eyes closed tightly, waiting for the dog to tear her apart. But it did not happen. Slowly she opened her eyes, and she saw a black dog howling and wagging its tail. Her eyes widened: It was Rex, her son David's dog. A spark of hope kindled in her heart. Rex had lived with her since he was a puppy until she'd had to give him away. But she didn't dare show any sign of recognition; she must not give away that they knew each other.

The officer ordered Rex to attack then remained silent, watching the dog. The dog's behavior puzzled and angered him. He had confiscated the dog from a Jewish family and taken him through training to erase his memory while implanting a hatred of Jews, teaching the shepherd to attack them viciously on command. But here, in front of this woman, he acted like a tame kitten.

Max pulled Rex's leash and repeatedly shouted the commands he'd taught him. Finally, the officer kicked him in frustration before reaching the idea that there was probably something special about that woman.

Chapter 18

Max barked at Rivka in German to come out of her hiding place. Rivka emerged trembling, afraid of what would happen to her. Max became conscious of Rivka's beauty through the neglect, through her shabby clothes, the accumulated dirt, the dried blood, and the nagging hunger in her cheeks. He lifted her chin with his bare knife. Rivka looked at him boldly.

"Where did you come from?" he asked Rivka in German.

She did not answer. Her only response was the welling of tears before they spilled.

He lay down the knife, grabbed her arm, and started leading her away. If he didn't kill her, he mustn't be seen talking to her like that. Something about the way the dog responded to this woman caused Max to soften just a bit. He ordered the woman to come along. Heinz, his brother-in-law, told him that he had found a Jewish girl and made her his sex slave and housemaid. Max thought Rivka might be a good candidate for such a position for him. With no other choice, Rivka obeyed and accompanied the German officer and his dog.

When they arrived at the officer's home, appropriated from a Polish family, Max gave her a gown, a towel, and a pair of warm socks. Next he showed her where the shower was.

Rivka entered the bathroom and closed the door behind her. She looked around at the signs of obvious neglect. Small insects that had come inside looking for refuge from the cold found their death in the cobwebs lingering in every corner. Would her fate be similar? To go from bad to worse? Rivka turned on the faucets, which coughed and spat out brown droplets. Finally, clear, icy water started flowing. She did not dare say a word. She took an old towel from a hook and lathered it with some industrial soap she found lying in the corner.

She washed her face and hair. Next, she took off her filthy, smelly blouse and washed her chest and under her arms. Then, she put on the robe and took off her wet pants, shoes, and socks that smelled of decay. She ran the cloth over the rest of her body quickly. She had no change of clothes, and so she left the room in the robe. On her feet she wore the warm socks and slippers that Max had given her. She closed her eyes and tried to hold on to this fraction of a second before transitioning to whatever might come next. Just the split second, when she felt relieved. Felt like a human again.

Stepping into the living room, she gathered the robe tightly around her, as if trying to protect herself with the thin layer of fabric. He was waiting for her with a cup of hot tea, a platter with lemons, sugar cubes, and cookies. Something in her melted at the sight of the refreshments.

"Sit down," he said in German.

Rivka didn't move.

Again Max said, "Sit down," this time in Polish and in a gentler tone. In his home he allowed himself to be less strict with the rules required of him as an officer. Rex, who had been sitting at Max's foot until then, got up and turned around. Rearing up on his hind legs, he wagged his tail towards Rivka. Max watched him from the corner of his eye.

Max poured Rivka a cup of tea and put it on the table. She sat down, took the cup of tea, and held it to warm her hands a little. Max looked at her, scrutinizing her up and down. This was a strange position for her to be in. To be regarded as a woman by a man after being considered subhuman for so long.

Rex finally calmed down and curled up in the space between her and Max. His body found the compromise between his loyalty to his old owner, Rivka, and his new loyalty to Max.

Rivka focused her gaze on the rising steam, blowing a bit on her tea to cool it and drinking carefully.

"I am Max," the officer said.

"Rivka," she replied.

Silence.

Max leaned across, this time with the plate of cookies. Rivka adopted a faint smile and took one as if breaking a long fast. When she finished she took another cookie and another one. Max watched her eat with a half-smile on his mouth.

Rivka felt uncomfortable under his gaze and pulled her robe tighter. Max did not have to explain much. Rivka knew exactly what he expected from her. A bitter lump sat in her throat, but she did not say a word. She flogged herself for not leaving with her children, but there wasn't even time for self-flagellation. She had to think fast.

Chapter 19

Rivka felt it wise not to give away her knowledge of the German language. Max decided to give Rivka a while to recover, to heal, and to fill out a little and put some meat on her bones. Then later, she would serve him. In every sense of the word.

He directed her into one of the bedrooms that he wasn't using. He left a pitcher of water, some fruit, and some toast in the room and encouraged her to rest, eat, and gain her energy back. He closed the door.

Rex scratched at the closed door a little, whined a bit, and finally, when Max scolded him, he curled up in front of the door as a guardian. Max kicked him to move him away, but Rex only got up and settled back down in a better position, his eyes alert. He did not budge. Max was confused by the dog's attitude towards the stranger.

Rivka moved around a little in the room, but fatigue soon overcame her. She climbed on the stiff mattress, covered up in the rough wool blanket and immediately fell asleep. She did not know how long she slept, and when she awoke she heard voices in German. Her heart was pounding. She remembered where she was, and she calmed slightly.

She tried to listen to the conversation in German and pressed her ear to the keyhole. Sometimes voices were muffled, and sometimes they were clear. She figured out that Max was talking with his assistant. Despite her weakness, the spy blood still ran through her veins, and she decided to collect as much information as she could.

Rivka was thoroughly on edge. The only thing that comforted her was her secret connection with Rex. A sort of hidden connection to her children. She tried to gather information about the outside world and about her fate. She listened to Max making jokes and mentioning her name in a quieter voice. She heard Max say goodbye to his assistant. Next the slamming of the door and then silence. She held her breath. However, no footsteps came her direction.

She walked around the room, like in a prison cell, checking every corner. She opened the closet, which was essentially a niche in the wall covered with wooden doors. On the bottom shelf Rivka found a pile of clothes that had been thrown there carelessly. There were clothes for a woman, a man, and children. She held the woman's clothes up in front of her. They weren't exactly flattering, but they'd do. In the end, she took off the robe and put on the clothes, which smelled slightly of mothballs.

Her eyes wandered around the meager room and settled

next on the dresser drawers. She went over and opened them. A pile of random paperwork spilled out. Some stamped post-cards. Signs of a normal life before the war. Kids' drawings. Suddenly her gaze rested on a thick brown leather album. She opened it and riffled through it, trying to identify the people in the photographs. Her eyes stopped on a class picture. She looked at it carefully and then it came to her it; it was the classroom where David had studied! Along with Laser!

How had she not recognized it before? She was in the home of Laser's family. Max had invaded it and apparently found Rex, who'd been left behind. Tears flowed from her eyes uncontrollably. Her whole body was overtaken by sobbing. The longing for her children pinched her and embittered her more than ever. Her body trembled and she collapsed on the floor.

"My David, my little boy... How could I abandon you like that? Look, I am getting my punishment ..." Her voice spoke to his image in a trembling whisper. She wiped her nose on her sleeve. "I promise you, I'm going to do everything — but everything — to see you again, my son..."

Rivka tore the picture out and hid it under her pillow. It was like receiving a message from her family, her son. She took it as a sign from heaven, that she must do everything she could, even at the cost of physical and mental humiliation, to get out of there and escape. She was determined to survive her stay under the same roof with a German monster at any price.

Chapter 20

Rivka wandered around the apartment trying to familiarize herself with her area of operation. Looking for vulnerabilities and mapping the terrain. When she got to the kitchen, she found jams in the cupboard that Laser's mother had preserved from the summer fruit — enough for the whole year. Among the other provisions, she found flour, oil, and sugar and decided to keep herself busy by baking. They had been stored well and weren't infested by insects thanks to the cold weather. The familiar routine of baking touched her soul, and she recalled the many happy occasions she had spent with Rakhel in the kitchen, creating pastries and other treats that pleased the whole family.

She knew she had only two options available: The first was to resist and suffer abuse, and the other was ostensibly to co-operate with the Nazi, Max, waiting for the right opportunity and then escaping.

She'd heard the rumors about the abuse of Jewish women by the Germans in the past. Her instincts guided her to take care of him and to succumb to his sexual demands. She hoped that then he'd let his guard down and she would be able to continue gathering information straight from the source.

Around dusk, Max came back with his dog. Rex jumped on Rivka and licked her in affection. Max still could not decipher this phenomenon, but his brow smoothed when he caught the aroma of her baking. His mouth began to water, but he waited patiently for the pastries to cool.

Rivka went into the living room, took off Max's shoes, and began to massage his feet, cold from the walk in the snow. She set the kettle to boil and filled a basin with salt and oil to soften the skin. She brought in the tub, rolled up his trousers, and dipped his feet in the warm water. The whole time she tried not to look up. Max stretched out in the armchair, and a sigh escaped his lips. Finally, he felt, there was someone who would smooth the edges of his hard day. His military discipline required that he overcome any difficulties and function like a machine. He had a job to do and strict orders to follow.

Rivka took her time on the corns and the rough skin, as if this were Max's shell she could soften so a human side would come out and be kind to her. All the while she had a clear goal: to escape to the woods and join the partisans who could smuggle her to Israel, where she would be able to make plans to reunite with her family in America.

Every morning, Max locked Rivka in the house with the dog, but not before warning her to keep absolutely silent: "You better not be heard by the German neighbors."

Those were Germans who had also taken over the apartments of Jews who had been evacuated to camps. He made sure to frighten her by saying if she was discovered, she should expect to be physically and mentally abused until it killed her.

Usually in the mornings after she was left alone in the apartment, Rivka fell into a long sleep. She was exhausted from the difficult nights, in which Max would come to her room and have his way with her. The disgust that pervaded her along with his rumbling snores kept her awake. Rivka was determined to escape from the house — her prison — and to do so, she had to make Max think she had gotten used to him. She decided to feign collaboration and when he got into bed with her she would close her eyes and imagine that she was with Menachem. Max felt the change but said nothing.

Her knowledge of German allowed her to read the documents that Max often left on the table. She listened carefully while she was cleaning the house to his conversations with his assistant, who came every morning. That way she was aware of what the Nazis in the area were planning each day.

One morning, she heard a ticking noise coming from another bedroom. She opened the door carefully and saw a large teleprinter on the dresser; it was emitting documents in German one after the other. With her sharp instincts, she realized that she had a first-rate intelligence source. Using her excellent photographic memory and the content encryption method she'd used to fabricate the crossword puzzles for the underground, she began to gather information and store it.

She also knew that there must be an organized folder of messages that had arrived for Max before then. She immediately searched the room. She found a treasure trove in the folders that were neatly boxed in the corner.

Rivka knew instantly that she had to go through the extensive material as quickly as possible and that she might need more than one or two days for this operation.

She learned about the number of people who had been sent to their deaths at Treblinka. She shuddered when she heard Max and his assistant joke about how they enticed Jews to get on the trains with a slice of bread and some jam. She was nauseated when she thought about her brothers and sisters languishing in the ghetto. She thought about them being sent, unknowing, to their deaths like lambs to the slaughter. She clung to the knowledge that Yaakov's wisdom had prevented her children from that fate. She was determined to see them again.

Her method of encrypting information through crossword puzzles was proving successful in Max's home. She found paper and pencils and drew squares with vertical and horizontal lines filled with fabricated definitions. Within the solutions, she put the coded information she had learned. To anyone but Rivka it would seem like an intellectual hobby to pass the time.

She had to get to the forest and forward the vital information she had gathered.

As the days went by, Max's trust and confidence in Rivka grew and he would leave the apartment for two or three days asking Rivka to take care of the dog without attracting any attention. She was an expert at conducting herself so no one would guess anyone was in the apartment. She didn't turn the lights on in the evening and certainly not the music either, and she was careful not to bake pastries that smelled from afar. Max told his assistant that he didn't have to worry about the dog because his neighbors had promised to take care of him. Rex's company relieved her loneliness, and after she was left alone twice with the dog, she realized that this was her chance to take action. She decided that on Max's next trip she would escape.

***

Rivka found a screwdriver in a drawer in her room and tried to chisel around the door lock with it. Her progress was painfully slow. She had to keep quiet, and the tool in her hand was too small for the task. Her hands swelled and blistered, but she had to continue. Perspiration beaded on her forehead, and the fear the she didn't have sufficient time to break the lock before Max returned, brought her to paralysis and despair at times. She was afraid that he would punish her severely or even kill her. After a short pause, she collected herself and continued the job with determination and dedication. A long time went by, and though it was hard work, finally some light had seeped between the door and the frame. For her this was the light of hope.

Chapter 21

The light that came in seemed to cleanse Rivka from the inside out and created a renewed flow of energy in her. She vigorously continued to dig. With every fragment that fell out of the wall she felt the end approaching and she was filled with cautious optimism. After several more minutes the lock was freed and the door opened. Rex had sat beside her while she worked, watching her curiously with a sideways glance. When the door opened, he understood that she was about to leave, and he began to whine and lick her. Rivka contemplated whether to take him with her. She was afraid he might give her away. On the other hand, Rex had not only saved her life, he was in a way a souvenir from her son. She decided to repay him.

She wrapped herself in a scarf she found in her room and began walking towards the woods in the dark. The way was slow and difficult, and the road just went on and on. Rex stuck to her side with his ears raised, walking when she walked and stopping when she stopped. When her legs failed, he nuzzled at her and licked her hand. This encouraged her and helped her to carry on. She was terribly thirsty. Rex often stopped and licked remnants of thawed snow on the ground. Rivka did the same.

Rex's ears twitched. A hubbub of German reached her. Rivka looked quickly in all directions and found a wall to hide behind, crouched close to the ground. She tried to blend into the background like a chameleon camouflaged in a mosaic of gray and brown.

Rex barked as loud as he could and sent her heart beating like crazy. The next sound was a loud gunshot. Rex collapsed. The drunk German who shot him joked and bragged about his skill with his weapon as he walked past her hiding place with his two drunk friends. The pungent smell of alcohol wafted from them. She could hardly hold back the whimper that wanted to escape her. Almost silently she cried for the dog, for herself, and for her family. Fortunately, the rowdy voices of the Germans eclipsed any sound she might have made.

Rivka remained in the hiding place for many minutes until she could no longer hear the drunkards. Finally, her calm returned. Rex's death was a hard blow, but it confirmed her conviction that she let nothing stop her. Her determination only grew.

Rivka was tense and very tired. She moved slowly with a mournful spirit. She decided to find a place of shelter to rest. When she arrived at the first cluster of bushes between the forest trees, she lay down and curled up. Her head rested on the little bundle she had taken with her — she'd found a table-cloth in which she put a few cookies she'd baked along with some dry bread.

Like every other night when she tried to sleep, her mind ran over the events she'd experienced since her family left Poland: the work, the loneliness, and Menachem's visits. She watched these events as if they had happened to someone else. She loved falling asleep thinking about being embraced by Menachem's strong arms and masculine body. Her sleep was light, she was very tense, but the smile never left her lips — she could feel his caresses over her body.

She awoke to rhythmic taps on her shoulder and imme-diately understood that it wasn't Menachem's touch but a stranger's. Kind, bright blue eyes looked at her. She felt em-barrassed, as if caught in the act. The stranger sensed her dis-comfort. He told her that he was a partisan.

"Now you are in good hands," he assured her. "We will help you hide from the Germans, and perhaps we can extricate you to Palestine."

A smile of gratitude reached her lips. Relieved, she stood up. She met his comrades and nodded her thanks at them as they led her through the woods to a cabin. The tiny build-ing was well hidden in the branches and blended in perfectly with the landscape of the forest.

In the evening, to warm up, they lit a small fire in a hole that had been dug in the center of the cabin's dirt floor. Rivka stared at the fire. The orange flames dancing up and down and the glowing coals below hypnotized her. Finally, she was able to relax a little. Her body needed some respite from her endless vigilance, and Rivka felt fatigue and weariness wash through her in the heat of the fire. She felt safe enough in the woods among the partisans to rest for a while, and give her body the chance to recharge it desperately needed.

The next morning, she asked to speak with the commander of the partisan platoon. Rivka handed him the folded pieces of paper she had concealed in a hidden pocket she'd sewn in her dress.

"Before this all began, I was trained to encrypt information in crossword puzzles for the Jewish underground. You can find all the information I have gathered in the definitions."

The commander took them. "How do you know that the information is reliable?" He asked.

Rivka's throat closed up when she thought about what she had endured with Max, but she quickly recovered. "I was a prisoner in the house of a German officer who didn't know that I speak German. I have intelligence skills. Let me help you here as much as I can until you can put me on a boat to Palestine."

The commander thanked her, nodded, and walked away.

***

The Judenrat tried to convince the inhabitants of the ghetto to cease their protests and to cooperate with the Germans as long as they thought they could survive the ghetto somehow. When the council leaders finally understood where the Jews were being sent, they refused to cooperate and committed suicide. The ghetto slowly emptied. From severe overcrowding to low occupancy. The Jews who remained were ashamed to look in each other's eyes, contrite that they were still alive. When they realized that their deaths were unavoidable if sent to Treblinka, the uprising of the Warsaw ghetto began. In order to revolt, there was an urgent need for weapons, and the Jews were assisted by the Polish underground in smuggling weapons into the ghetto. They were able to get to these stockpiles of weapons with the information gathered by Rivka.

Chapter 22

Rivka met other refugees like her in the forest. Some of them she knew. They were torn and tattered, tired from their journeys. They were all jumpy from the constant vigilance that had kept them alive. Their only possessions were the clothes they wore. She looked at them and then at herself. She examined her dress and her thick wool leggings, and the number of holes in them and wondered how long they would last.

The partisans didn't want to promise anything at first. Although Jews had been smuggled in the past, during the war the difficulties in procuring a ship were enormous. While the refugees waited, hunger and thirst prevailed and supplies were scarce. Finally, a rumor reached them that offered some hope: The partisans talked about a ship that was to arrive to collect them. They were warned to be patient, quiet, and discreet and to try and bear up under the hunger, the thirst, and the cold. Rivka found some thin, flexible tree bark. She perforated holes for her eyes and nose and wore it as a mask. This way she prevented the chapping of her lips and skin from the cold. Others tied handkerchiefs and scarves on their faces and looked like mummies.

One night a messenger gave them a promising message: "The ship has arrived." He wore a black coat, but his collar points were an angel's wings. He asked them to get up and accompany him to the port. The refugees rose in exemplary silence. Their figures in the dark were more like shadows than people — long-suffering and emaciated. Their only meager possessions on their bodies, but a little cheer finally sprouted in their hearts.

The overcrowding on the boat was unbearable. The starving refugees pushed and shoved for food and water. The fittest took over the bunks where there was a window or an opening. There were some who took another's piece of bread. Later they felt ashamed, but between shame and hunger, the latter spoke more loudly.

Seasickness made them vomit violently. Crowding, chaos, the stench of the vomit, no change of clothes. The refugees were not allowed to go out on the deck during the day, so they remained in the belly of the ship, where the dense, closed conditions were a fertile breeding ground for bacteria and disease. The squalor and the wretchedness brought them frequently to despair. Rivka was grateful that this journey was already over for her children and was horrified to imagine what they had suffered. Maybe an adult could carry all this, but a child? A child cannot control hunger. Rivka shivered when she watched a child die and his body released into the water. She chased away fantasies of her children, and she consoled herself with the idea that when they'd left, Europe was less desperate.

A woman who gave birth on board to a boy died immediately after. The captain did her the honor of wrapping her body in an elegant blue and white flag, and his crew sent her body over the side. The captain told the stunned husband, "She died as a daughter of Israel, and your son will live as a free man."

Another birth ignited a glimmer of optimism in the eyes of the refugees. The terrible heat and the lack of food and water did not nourish the mother enough to breastfeed her baby. So she made a makeshift pacifier, dipped it in water and let him suck on it. A life jacket was put into a basket and used as a mattress for the newborn; torn shirts became diapers. Miraculously, he survived.

As evening came, the ship approached land, and the shores of the Promised Land were seen from afar. They had to exercise caution. Rivka knew how rare it was to succeed where many had failed, were caught, or never left at all. In the middle of the night, they docked near the port of Jaffa and the passengers were transferred into smaller boats that could reach the beach. For Rivka, the transition from the hell of the crowded ship to the open air of the Promised Land was like touching the gates of heaven. She felt the slap of the salty ocean on her face and hands and the night breeze caressing her hair and she opened her arms wide. The salty water droplets mixed with her salty tears. Relief, release, euphoria, and grief flavored it all. Her lips whispered a prayer: "*Ken yehi ratzon*... Amen."

Chapter 23

The British sent the refugees to a camp in Atlit, although some were delayed for arrest. The men were separated from the women. Upon their arrival, they were disinfected with DDT. After, Rivka walked slowly among the modest wood huts. The wind caught her hair, and she looked up at the sky and smiled to herself. *Soon. Soon*, she thought. This delay didn't break her spirit, and she could smell the freedom.

Several hundred refugees were housed in the camp. Rivka's secretive eyes and attentive ears were alert for any piece of information she could learn by walking among the British guards who lived with their families there. A Hebrew newspaper sitting on a table in one of the offices caught her eye. She understood from the article that the Brits were being pressured to release them. "Eleanor Rathbone asked the deputy minister to ensure that there is no intention to force these refugees to migrate further from Israel." So said the news. Rivka was pleased and she savored this information.

Alongside the Jewish refugees who had sailed from

Romania, there were immigrants from Yemen and Algeria. Rivka was fascinated by the gathering of the cultures that would form her new country. Others were more concerned with the fact that their hardship did not seem at an end. The British policy on immigration into Palestine was very tough. Uncertainty welled in their hearts. The knowledge that they were in the land of their dreams, the reasonable conditions in which they lived and the adequate food and water kept Rivka and her refugee friends comfortable and hopeful they would be released.

One morning, Moshe Shertok went to Atlit. He was the head of the political department of the Jewish agency that acted as the ministry of foreign affairs for the Jewish settlement in the country. His ties with the British Mandate allowed him to visit the camp. Quickly, a swarm of people crowded around him. His appearance was like a breeze of hope for them. He talked to them and encouraged them.

Rivka believed all was not lost. She saw Shertok's visit as a sign and another milestone in the odyssey of her hardship — another step towards her children, whom she pictured every night before bed.

Initially, she was assigned to do odd jobs in the camp, but after they were split into teams, and thanks to the many languages she spoke, Rivka was referred to an office in Tel Aviv. There she sorted and translated documents. Rivka learned that in Tel Aviv there were many underground organizations. She still didn't know how to channel this information, but her talent for stealth from her spy days and the habit of information gathering stayed with her.

At the end of each workday she returned to her room. Naomi, with whom she shared the room, was friendly and cordial and loved to talk. Rivka responded with affection as well. They lived in a rented room in the apartment of an elderly widow. The old woman was hard of hearing. This was a clear benefit for the young women, in that it assured she would never interfere or be interested in their actions. Sometimes Naomi and Rivka took walks together on the beach. They even went to the Eden movie theater together and on beautiful evenings watched movies under the stars, side by side.

Rivka never shared her past with Naomi or the others who were a part of her life in Palestine. She told no one about her family and her children. She wasn't ready to get that close to anyone.

PART FOUR: MENACHEM

Chapter 24

November 29, 1947. That day was the happiest ever for Menachem. On that day the United Nations declared the establishment of the State of Israel. Immediately after the votes were counted at the General Assembly of the UN, Menachem went out to the streets dancing with the rest of Israel. It was a moment of ecstasy he had been waiting for during his underground years. The triumph was so great that it even brought relief from his fevered thoughts of Rivka. He did not think of a single thing while he danced like a madman, drunk and happy, until the crack of dawn.

But when he went to sleep at first light, the gloom fell over him again. Menachem couldn't stop thinking about Rivka. During the breaks in his clandestine activities, her image had always snuck into his mind. He was worried and vexed by uncertainty over what had happened to her. He knew that the Jews of Europe were subjected to violence, exile, persecution, cold, hunger, and countless other dangers. She hadn't left his mind for many years.

His love remained in his heart, but the one he loved had vanished. He recruited his friends in the underground who were still scattered across Europe to try and find his beloved. The identifying details he had were her address, her description, and the description of her parents. For a long time, these facts led nowhere. Rivka and her parents could not be found.

Gradually, word began to arrive from his friends in Europe. The information was devastating. The story about the shooting in the town square, where Rivka and her parents were probably killed, came from different sources. Menachem realized bitterly that Rivka had probably perished along with her parents and all of the town's Jews in a Nazi roundup. From then on, sorrow had accompanied him wherever he turned.

But he didn't have much time for a battered soul.

After a few hours of sleep, after the adrenaline wore off, he was called to help strengthen the Haganah forces. The British were about to depart, and it was already clear there was a war coming. His underground experience had served him well in combat even before the official founding of the state. Immediately after establishing the State of Israel, the underground organizations, primarily the Haganah, became the Israeli Defense Forces. This was the official and regulated army in charge of the defense and the security of the young country. Menachem was appointed an officer.

After a while, he was offered the position of military attaché in the United States in charge of acquiring weapons for the new nation. After some hesitation, he accepted.

"The only thing that bothers me is being separated from my little sister. We are orphans, and my job is to keep her safe and to take care of her."

"The country is more important than any one family or individual," his commander replied.

"Yes, but since our parents had passed, our relationship has become closer and we each other's rock."

"You have to leave tonight," the commander demanded. It was not only a demand; it was an order.

But Menachem did not give up, and before leaving on his mission, he went to visit his sister, Leah, who lived in a kibbutz in the north of Israel. Menachem arrived at the kibbutz early in the evening and immediately headed to his sister's room. There he found Leah and Joseph embracing. Menachem was so surprised that his tongue stuck to his palate. Leah broke free of Joseph's arms and announced that Joseph had proposed to her and they were in fact just waiting for his approval.

"Give us your blessing," Leah asked.

Menachem was excited, and he moved his head to look at each of them in turn. He was very fond of Joseph, and he remembered that in the time they had spent together as children, Leah was always with Joseph. Their relationship was apparently stronger than he had realized.

Menachem asked Joseph about his past and his family. For the first time in all their years of friendship, Joseph mentioned his parents. He never talked about them, and when he'd come to the kibbutz at the age of fifteen, he'd said he was an orphan. The other children were very careful not to ask about them so as not to hurt him.

"I was born to an orthodox family, the fourth generation in Jerusalem," he began. "My great-grandfather was a watchmaker who passed along his skills and profession to my grandfather and then to my father. I broke the line. I had no interest in the Torah or in watch springs."

Joseph lowered his eyes and stopped talking. Tears ran down his cheeks. Leah felt his pain and took his hand.

"I left my parents in Jerusalem and came to this kibbutz," Joseph continued. "It wasn't easy to live faithless in an orthodox society and even more difficult to tell that to my father and mother. One day, I left them a letter, as that was the only way I saw fit, and I disappeared. I told no one that I had parents, and so I was treated as an orphan. All contact with my family was lost. I'm sure I deeply hurt them."

Menachem gathered Leah and Joseph in a powerful embrace of spiritual togetherness. After that he could no longer put off the reason for his visit. He told his sister he was to be the first military attaché at the Israeli Embassy in the United States. He shared his concerns with her and Joseph. Leah reassured him that the pain of their past had eased. She told her brother that Joseph helped her to be stronger and that he should not worry. She was in good hands, and soon they would marry and have a family of their own.

Menachem's face fell when he realized he would not be available to walk her down the aisle. Leah hugged him lovingly. She knew how much her brother loved and worried about her. She reminded her brother that from then on Joseph would be by her side. She assured Menachem that she knew he would be there in spirit on the happiest day of her life. They talked for a while longer before Menachem went on his way with mixed feelings of relief and heartache.

Chapter 25

Menachem landed in New York after a long ocean crossing. Through the many nights he had rocked on the waves, lying on his bed thinking about his life — about Rivka and his sister whom he had left behind. Finally, he arrived in New York Harbor, where the First Lady of Liberty greeted him with blessings.

He moved into an apartment that had been prepared for him in advance, but he tried to be at the lonely apartment as little as possible. He worked late almost every day, busy with meetings and assignments, and in the evenings he would return home and quickly drop off to sleep.

He missed his sister very much and tried to picture her wedding. *There is still time*, he thought. Menachem decided to surprise his sister by sending her a dowry package from America. It was the very least he could do as her only older brother, whose absence would shout to the skies at the wedding ceremony.

Menachem went into a department store. The store had

multiple floors; he had never seen such wealth and abundance. *Everything is big in America*, he thought.

Because he needed a few things from each floor and as a typical man he wasn't familiar with what to buy a woman, he asked for the help of a young, attractive saleswoman. The scent of perfume drifted around her. More than one scent in fact. She was like a cosmetics model from top to bottom. In a blue suit and crimson shawl, with blood-red lips, she looked like a walking advertisement. She also wore a wide smile, glad to be of help to such a handsome man.

She chatted comfortably and asked for whom he was buying the wedding dress. He noticed that her smile brightened when he told her it was a gift for his sister overseas. Menachem was not oblivious; he understood clearly that she was flirting with him. But he didn't feel a strong need for a woman's company. His heart still ached for his beloved Rivka. Meanwhile, the saleswoman was excited by the opportunity to earn a fat commission by helping a stranger spend his money in this huge department store. He spent a substantial amount of money on Leah's dowry, selecting a wedding dress, bedding, towels, and fine undergarments. He hoped that she would be happy with his gift, rather than sad at his absence.

When Menachem was ready to leave, the saleswoman seemed slightly disappointed that he only thanked her politely for her assistance and made no further conversation. She apparently had confused his friendliness for something more.

The next morning, he rushed to the local post office to

send the package. He stood in line studying the magnificent building. Again, he thought about the great splendor prevailing everywhere, compared to the poverty of the land of Israel. Nevertheless, his heart longed for his homeland.

When he reached the counter he set the box down and, before looking up said, "I have to send this package to Israel." He lifted his head, and when his gaze met the clerk's eyes, his breath caught and his heart raced. The pretty clerk made him weak in the knees. The girl on the other side of the counter was the exact replica of his beloved Rivka. He blushed and his hands shook as he paid for the package. He could not find words, so he nodded his thanks and walked away quickly.

Chapter 26

The girl at the post office awoke dormant sensations in Menachem. Especially his feelings as a man. That night, he tossed and turned, having nightmares about Rivka, about the girl. Sweaty erotic dreams and dreams of persecution and yelling. He was torn up inside. His heart belonged to Rivka, but the girl had aroused him. Women found him attractive. They liked him, wanted him, and many were quite bold in their attentions. Until this woman, he had not felt anything in return. His heart was cold, as if he had given all his love to Rivka and there was nothing more left.

Menachem found himself coming up with excuses to go to the post office. Once he bought stamps, another time he asked for information about post office boxes, and a different time he checked the options for shipping by weight.

Finally, he realized that this attraction was stronger than him. In his heart, he asked for forgiveness from Rivka, assuring her that she would always remain his first love. One day, he mustered the courage to ask Rachel, the post office clerk, for dinner. She accepted the invitation.

Her blue eyes shone with the same spark that he'd seen in Rivka's eyes, and Menachem could not avoid the comparison. Her English was perfect and unaccented; he believed she was a native and so he asked her to help him learn his way around.

Rachel was lonely and found comfort in Menachem. Her days were spent working in the post office, and in the evening she traveled more than an hour to the apartment where she lived with her father. She barely managed to live on her salary, as the bulk of it went to pay the rent. She often found him lying in bed, in a stupor, mumbling the names of his missing loved ones — his wife, his children, his sister, and her family.

As his condition worsened, Rachel did her best to nurse him and feed him, but in the end he was beyond her help. His liver had been severely damaged from the endless drinking. And one day when Rachel returned from work, her father would not wake up. He was huddled on the edge of his bed, a bottle on the floor, the sheets wild and filthy, and alone, in exile, he returned his soul to the Creator.

After her father's death Rachel withdrew even further into herself. After leaving Poland she had refused to speak Polish and only spoke it with her father. On her own after his passing, she spoke only English. The little Hebrew she had learned had been forgotten.

It was under those circumstances that she met Menachem. Their common loneliness and grief brought them together.

Menachem would come to the post office at the end of his

workday and pick her up. They ate together and took long walks. Rachel showed him her favorite New York spots. One day, as they watched the squirrels cavorting in Central Park, he drew her close and kissed her. After, they nestled together, finding in one another the warmth they both missed so much.

PART FIVE: RIVKA

Chapter 27

Rivka got up to another day of work. She looked in the mirror — dark circles surrounded her eyes. She washed her face with cold water to fully wake up. Cold water shrinks the blood vessels around the eyes, she remembered her mother saying.

As if the European ways had stayed with her, she had been but a shadow of herself for so long. Of a human. Now she was free, and she enjoyed the right to stand quietly in front of the mirror in the morning.

She powdered her nose and her eyes, smeared lipstick on her lips, and left for the office. She tried to hide the signs of the frenzied nights she had — nights filled with fragmented images that give her no rest.

She sees her elderly parents walking hand in hand down the street, her father's head held high. And the Nazis see it. They bully him and cut off his side curls, his yarmulke is knocked from his head again and again and yet he keeps walking, proudly reciting, "*Sh'ma Yisrael ….*"

Her father collapses from the butt of a rifle; her mother

screams and bends over him, and she too takes a blow from the same gun. Rivka holds in her scream by biting her lower lip. She is exploding inside.

Her parents' bodies are on the ground side by side, a blink before everyone else is shot, and Rivka collapses underneath them.

Nausea hits her when she realizes that she is the only one left, and she needs to stay there in between the bodies in order to survive.

The sleeplessness had started to show. In front of the mirror, she saw the thin red blood vessels that crossed the whites of her eyes so that even from afar they looked pink. She was starting to unravel. The maddening nights became the center and the days were unremembered.

On good nights, Menachem featured in her dreams. On those occasions, Rivka directed all her energy towards him at night and the next day she was left empty. The memories were vivid snapshots: Menachem fixing her window. Menachem learning Polish and trying to teach her a phrase in Moroccan but in vain. Menachem laughing over a morning cup of coffee.

Her only connection to reality was her job. She sat in her office and translated documents. It was often hard for her to concentrate. Sometimes she'd fall asleep at her desk only to be woken by her own muttering minutes later.

She always pulled herself together and carried on. She had never given up on seeing her children again, but the connection had become more tenuous. Her spirit failed, and she fell into a melancholy routine.

Once in a while the pressure cooker of her feelings released in a heart-wrenching wail. *What a stupid, colossal mistake I made! What was I thinking when I let my children leave without me? What tortures I went through. Was it all worth it? For what? To sit here and translate documents?* "Where are my parents? Where are my children? Where is Menachem? You all left me," she cried out. The sound of her own voice startled her.

She lifted her head and looked around hoping no one had heard, and her eyes settled on a handsome man standing in the doorway. Rivka organized her papers and patted her hair, embarrassed that he'd witnessed her grief. In her awkwardness she looked like a little girl.

Chapter 28

Walter walked into the office and smiled. He was a handsome, impressive man, younger than Rivka. He came to the office every other week with a briefcase full of documents for translation. Their eyes met. Rivka smiled at him shyly. Something about the vulnerability she radiated along with her beauty captured Walter. He felt as if he could stare forever into her light blue eyes. Her cheeks and nose were decorated with freckles, a gift from her sunny new country. Little wrinkles around the eyes were common in a country where plants wither and die early. Even younger women displayed such creases.

"Your presence I fancy, lovely maiden. Or in other words, you are beautiful." Walter bowed deeply after he spoke and rose with a charming grin.

Rivka smiled modestly in return. She realized how transparent she was even though she tried so hard in the mornings to cover up behind the powder. She was like an open book for him.

His kind words were just what she needed right then: comfort from a friend. His warmth gave her relief from her despondency.

"Would you like something to drink?" she offered.

"Gladly," he replied.

Rivka made tea with lemon for both of them. The kind that reminded her of her childhood. They sipped their tea in silence for a few minutes, avoiding eye contact out of mild embarrassment.

"Great flavor," Walter said finally, always ready with a compliment at any opportunity.

"Thank you." She smiled. "This is nothing; you need to see what else I can make. Next time, let me know in advance when you are coming and I promise to make you some homemade sweets."

"I will do so for sure." Walter was pleased by her kindness and her offer and looked forward to seeing her again.

He left Rivka's office and walked happily through the streets of Tel Aviv. He walked down Sheinkin Street thinking about the woman who lit up his senses. On the right he saw the offices of the *Davar* newspaper. Up ahead was the Sheinkin Street grove and as he daydreamed, he eyes passed over the central synagogue of the neighborhood. Walter noticed none of these things, only Rivka was in his heart and mind.

For his next visit, as promised, Rivka brought in some baked goods she hadn't prepared in a while. He asked her what was the special ingredient she used. The main ingredient was longing, she thought.

"What a wonderful flavor! Sweet as honey!" Walter announced, and Rivka blushed. "Have you ever been to Café Filtz?" Walter asked.

"No, I have not," Rivka replied.

And so Walter took her by the hand and together they went out to lunch in the café on the beach.

She was surprised to see that people at the café weren't in khaki uniform. They were met by staff dressed in fancy evening clothes, tuxedos, and bow ties even at that hour.

"It's like Europe," Rivka said, unable to hide her glee.

For a while, she reveled in the Europe she used to know before everything fell apart. She looked at a man at the next table and noted that he was dressed in an elegant suit. She looked down at herself and became uncomfortable. All the men were dressed in white, buttoned shirts and dark ties. The women had exposed backs, exposed ankles, and wore beautiful dresses. One woman sat in an ornate embroidered gown as if a dance were starting soon. Rivka was flustered among the bourgeoisie. She looked at the pants and white shoes she wore, and hid them under the table.

Walter brought his head to her neck and breathed deeply of her fragrance. "I no longer know what has a better aroma, your pastries or you. Your scent is intoxicating, and I could drift away in the flowers in your hair."

Rivka found his nearness a little disquieting for she was terribly conflicted. A battle was taking place inside her. Guilt spearheaded the struggle. Feelings of betrayal of her family and her beloved Menachem, and the fact that handsome Walter was years younger than her, clashed with her desire for closeness, comfort, and warmth.

In the end, Rivka remembered that she was a woman, and he had awoken something in her dormant for so long. The longing for a man, a lover, for Menachem, a warm shoulder overwhelmed all her attempts to repel intimate relations with a man. The passion in her won the contest, and she finally gave in to her feelings and invited Walter back to her apartment. She knew that the apartment would be empty because Naomi had told her that morning that she wouldn't be coming home that night. She was a nurse at the Hadassah Hospital and had signed on for a double shift.

As soon as the door closed behind them, all the barriers broke. The looks, touches, and caresses of their initial relationship erupted into a volcano without restraint. Rivka's mental and physical hunger were expressed in the intensity of her body's needs. She merged with Walter's body perfectly. Her whole being shivered at his touch on her back, hips, and neck. Finally, when he penetrated her, Rivka felt that they were one, moving in perfect harmony, and so they fell asleep in each other's arms.

Chapter 29

A playful sunbeam hit Rivka's face and awoke her. She opened her eyes slowly as a pleasant sensation engulfed her. She had no need to rush anywhere. She turned on her side, and was rewarded with a lovely view. Walter was lying beside her, his hair tousled, half his face squashed against the pillow, and his saliva drooling out of his mouth. Despite all that, in the early morning hours, he was beautiful to her.

Rivka glanced at the clock on the wall. She had to get to work! She slipped quietly into the bathroom to wash her face. While she splashed cold water on herself, she paused to look at her reflection in the mirror. Tiny lines that weren't usually visible to the naked eye seemed deeper than ever. She was convinced her guilt had manifested itself in the wrinkles on her face.

Rivka rushed to the toilet and vomited as her stomach continued to cramp. Her ignorance of the fate of her family, or the fate of her beloved Menachem fought with her irresponsible hedonism of the night before, grabbing her by the belly and shaking her up. She returned to the bedroom worn like a rag, but clean. Inside and out. She made a decision that this would be a one-time event, and she wouldn't see Walter anymore. She decided to break it to him very gently, and so she waited for the right opening.

Walter got up slowly and smiled at her, all disheveled. He saw that she was already dressed and ready for the new day. He crossed to the bathroom, stopping at her side for a kiss on the cheek. With a smile, she hurried him along to the bathroom.

Rivka packed her bag, and when Walter returned she told him she had to rush to the office, and Naomi would return soon, so they'd better leave at once. Finally, they stood in the doorway fully dressed. Walter kissed her neck. She felt this wasn't the time or the place to share her decision, but she felt her body grow rigid at his touch.

"The wait till I see you again will be hard on me," Walter whispered to her, his happiness shining through his words. "Being around you lifts me up … I hope that time flies between now and our next meeting." He hugged her and kissed her cheek again. "I have to leave for a few weeks, but as soon as I get back, I'll come and visit you."

Rivka forced a smile, impatient to send him on his way.

Chapter 30

Rivka fumbled in the folder for documents that she needed to translate. She grabbed a pile and brought it to her desk with a steaming cup of tea. When she sat down, a woman who looked vaguely familiar came into her office. The blond woman wore a coarsely woven brown skirt suit woven. Something about her reminded Rivka of Europe, of her hometown.

Rivka welcomed the stranger and offered her a cup of tea and a cookie. While conversing over tea, Rivka introduced herself. The woman intrigued her, for no reason she could put her finger on.

"My name is Bilhah," the woman introduced herself. She told Rivka that she had studied in the town of Nadvorna in Poland.

"Nadvorna?" Rivka asked excitedly. "I thought I recognized you. We studied at the same school!"

Excited by the revelation, they talked about the past. They chattered quickly as if they would never be able to catch up.

Rivka requested permission to leave work early and invited

Bilhah to take a walk around town. That way they could chat undisturbed and have enough time to enjoy such a rare reunion. Rivka felt she had received a blessing from home — The woman came from her hometown, after all!

They strolled and chatted for hours, updating each other on all that had happened to them and their families in the years since they had parted. Finally, Rivka told another living soul what had happened to her. Who else could understand her like someone from her city? She spoke of the *aktzia* — the roundup — in Warsaw Square.

"On the one hand I am happy that my children did not have to go through that horror. On the other hand I grieve for my parents and regret my decision to stay behind. Now I am left alone." A whimper refused to stay in Rivka's throat. It came out slowly at first and then intensely at full force. "All I wanted was to support my parents in their old age. Now my parents are gone, and my children, I do not know where they are and whether they are okay."

Bilhah hugged her and comforted her. Rivka didn't mention Menachem.

"I thought that when I got to Israel my loneliness would end. I went through so many hardships on my way here. Now, I work, and the daily routine brings no consolation for the absence of my children. What else do I have to go through in this life? Have I not suffered enough?"

Bilhah felt that her old schoolmate Rivka needed her, that it would be good to be together and to console each other for their losses, and also to remember together the things they'd loved and lost in their hometown. It was clear that Rivka, given her emotional state, should not be left so lonely in the big city.

"Why don't you come to visit me on holiday in the kibbutz?" Bilhah asked. "The fresh air will be good for you. You'll eat fresh food, walk around the kibbutz trails, pick fruit straight from the tree, and mainly be in a loving environment where you can get some rest. What do you think?"

"I do not want to be a burden," Rivka replied, wiping the leftover tears from her face. The very suggestion had already brought her some solace.

"Nonsense. I need your company just as much. Come rest. If you like it, I'll see how you can become a kibbutz member. That way you can contribute more to the Zionist dream than you can by translating documents in a dark office. We are about to hold a wedding in the kibbutz. You have never experienced such festivity. What do you say?"

Rivka saw an opportunity for a change and a gentle way to end her relationship with Walter. "All right," Rivka responded to the invitation, "but only if you let me help in the household chores."

She marveled at the ways of the Creator, and the blessings that are bestowed on His people.

Chapter 31

Joseph's eyes sparkled as he gazed at Leah under the *chuppah*. He was dressed to the nines, and Leah wore the wedding dress her brother had sent from New York. The bride was so beautiful, the groom wanted to savor the moment.

"*Harei 'at mekudeshet li* (Behold, you are consecrated to me)," he declared. Then taking her finger and slipping on the ring, but not all the way, Joseph very pointedly said: "*Betaba'at zo, kedat Moshe v'Yisrael* (by this ring, according to the ritual of Moses and Israel)." He raised his leg to break the wrapped glass.

Everyone in attendance stopped breathing momentarily when the groom said: "*Im eshkachech Yerushalayim, / Tishkach yemini./ Tid'bak leshoni lechiki, /Im-lo ezkereichi* (If I forget thee, O Jerusalem, / Let my right hand forget her cunning./ Let my tongue cleave to the roof of my mouth, / If I remember thee not)" and they waited to hear the glass shatter. And when Joseph brought down his foot, everyone broke into cheers. Another home was made in Israel and spirits were high.

All the members of the kibbutz attended the wedding, making the absence of Yoram and Menachem even more noticeable. The dining room tables were arranged in long rows for the buffet, and friends and neighbors had prepared their favorite dishes for the celebration. Vegetable pies and cheese balls wrapped in almond chips, *labne kefir* with genuine local olive oil and *za'atar* with toasted sesame seeds scattered lightly on top. The women had baked breads and made sure they had risen the previous night. Fish pulled from the depths of the nearby Mediterranean Sea the same day were grilled. Tomatoes were cut for the salad; orange juice was squeezed. The best foods of the land. Such a wealth of honoring was not often seen, especially in the early stages of a country that experienced so much upheaval and austerity. But here, among all the jubilation, the foods seemed appropriately festive. The singing and the dancing went on until the wee hours.

Rivka couldn't remember the last time she had danced and enjoyed herself like that. She returned to her room smiling. She removed her shoes, releasing her aching feet. She took off her skirt, which had lost its crease from the dancing. She snapped open the pin holding her hair and it fell on her shoulders caressing the faint lines that the sun seared on her skin. Her mind began to wander, and the images were alive before her again.

Yearning for her children, her parents, Rivka's eyes moistened and her tears smeared the black eyeliner as they found the wrinkles and the creases on her face the most convenient path to flow down. The air in the room was heavy, and it seemed that a monster lay waiting in the dark, thick air. A monster that wouldn't let go, especially when it found her alone.

As her mind continued to fret and wander, she realized that she did not know anything about Menachem except his first name. How could she find him without a surname or an address? Those thoughts were pushed aside by a deep remorse for the way she had treated Walter. She had simply disappeared without a trace.

Over the next couple of days, after her conscience calmed, she began to revel in the beauty of the trails, the trees and grass, the bustle of the dining room, and she savored her vacation. She was captivated by life on the kibbutz. On the surface, this place seemed a cure for her loneliness. Her employers in Tel Aviv agreed to waive her two-week notice, and she resigned immediately. She gathered her few belongings and wrapped up her life in the big city.

She found peace in working with children. The children in the kibbutz nursery shone light into her life. The clever and innocent sayings of the children, their purity, brought a smile to her face. At night she wandered the grounds, afraid to return to her room, afraid to not sleep again. Only at the point she was drunk with fatigue would she collapse on her bed, her eyes squeezed shut until morning.

Bilhah was glad that her friend had found some tranquility.

The two women enjoyed meeting from time to time as each returned to her own life. One night, Bilhah went out to pick some sage leaves and mint for tea, and she spotted Rivka across the way. She called her once, twice, and finally Rivka turned around casually then continued on her way. Bilhah returned home confused and wondered whether Rivka's transition to the kibbutz had strengthened or undermined her friend's mental state.

Bilhah felt a certain responsibility for Rivka's welfare because she had brought her there. She decided to turn to Giora, the kibbutz secretary, for advice.

Giora was dressed, as always, in khaki shorts. His long ear-to-ear mustache couldn't hide his constant smile. Sandals and cap completed the basic Israeli look. Indeed, Giora was one of the founders of the Palmach —the elite strike force of the Haganah — and the kibbutz. Giora listened intently to Bilhah and promised to visit Rivka in the evening and invited her to join him.

Giora knocked on Rivka's door, but she didn't respond. He saw that the light was on and opened the door slowly, continuing to knock. When they entered the room, they saw Rivka on the couch staring at the wall in front of her. Bilhah approached Rivka hesitantly. Before she reached the sofa, she had second thoughts and decided to give Giora some time alone with Rivka. She changed direction and went to the kitchen to brew a pot of tea. She served steaming tea to all of them and pulled the blanket around Rivka's shoulders.

"Rivka, we care about you. We want you to be happy here in the kibbutz," Giora said. "Bilhah came to me very concerned for you. How can we help you and improve your life here? You are so dedicated, and you have become an important part of our lives and the lives of our children. It's hard for us to see you like this ..."

Rivka just kept staring at the wall, holding her teacup. A few minutes later she took a sip from the cup warming her hands. It was a reflex, a habit she had brought from her cold country. But it brought her no relief; all she wanted was to drown in that teacup.

Bilhah tried again. "Darling, after all you went through — all the hardships, across continents and the sea, rescued from those who wished to kill you, only to want to die here in the country of your dreams!"

Rivka began to sob quietly.

Bilhah continued cautiously. "Darling, you have to at least try ... for your children. They are somewhere missing you!"

Rivka's silent weeping became a bitter cry. Slowly, she opened her heart: "There is no point to my life. I do not know where my beloveds are. My children. My parents are already gone. And the other people who have come my way and become dear to me, I have no way to reach them."

Giora tried to give her a reason to be optimistic. "You know, there is a radio program that deals with people just like you — people who have lost loved ones to the horror of the Holocaust — and they attempt to reconnect scattered families. 'Search Bureau for Missing Relatives' it's called. It airs every day on Kol Israel. I am sure that is your best chance to be reunited with your family. Miracles have happened with their help. A father found his son, a brother found his sister. I am sure you can also find your beloveds. You must hold on to the hope. To the thought that you will find whom you are looking for. Hold on to the vision."

For the first time since they entered, Rivka looked up.

"Even the State of Israel, without a vision of hope and perseverance, would not have come about. Am I right? I promise you that tomorrow morning I will give the radio show the details of your lost family. Maybe they have come to Israel from the United States, and maybe they do not know that you are alive or where you live."

A glimmer of a smile appeared on Rivka's lips. "Thank you," she muttered. She felt somewhat calmer, and the demons that lurked in the dark receded into the shadows.

She slept better that night, and from the next day on, she routinely listened to "Search Bureau for Missing Relatives" praying it would bring a miracle to her the way it had to others.

Chapter 32

After two weeks, Walter went to Rivka's office, just as he had promised. He was greeted by a woman whom he did not know, sitting in Rivka's chair.

"Might you know where Rivka is?" he asked gently.

"Unfortunately not," she replied. "She no longer works here."

"When did she leave? Did she leave an address?" A crease appeared between his eyebrows.

"I think two weeks ago. She left Tel Aviv but didn't say where she was going."

Walter left the package he'd brought with the woman and walked out of the office, deflated. He'd spent two weeks missing Rivka; now the object of his longing was gone and he had no way to find her.

In bed at night he often listened to the radio to relieve his loneliness. Heartsick, he tried to find diversion in the music. After his favorite show ended, the show called "Search Bureau for Missing Relatives" came on. Suddenly, an idea came to him, and he listened attentively. Hopefully. He heard mothers looking for children separated from them during the Holocaust, brothers looking for sisters, fathers for sons. Stories of happy reunions were also plentiful. Walter listened eagerly, praying he could find his Rivka.

He was so disappointed when he'd learned that Rivka disappeared leaving no trace. He could not begin to guess what had happened to her. What could it mean? He immediately felt a kinship with the families looking for loved ones, hoping to find them alive. He hoped for a miracle too, but every night at the end of the show he was disappointed, falling asleep in despair and with watery eyes.

One day he heard the announcer talking about a woman named Rivka. Although he knew nothing about her, he decided that it was a promising lead and worth pursuing. They said on the show that this Rivka lived on a kibbutz in the north of the country, and she was looking for her husband, Yaakov, and their children, Rakhel, David, and Laibel. The message was: "Anyone who has any information on the whereabouts of Rivka's family is asked to contact her or the kibbutz secretary."

After much deliberation, Walter decided to take a journey to the north to make contact with a stranger named Rivka or maybe his very own Rivka.

He left at dawn and traveled many hours on a bus. It was his first trip on the coastal highway since it was built and he could not have been more moved by the sight. The sun accompanied him all day until he watched it set through the bus windows. The beauty of the sunset only increased his melancholy. When Walter reached the kibbutz, he walked through the gates and was greeted by the sight of a farmer carrying tools on his back, returning from a hard day in the field.

"Please excuse me, sir!" Walter called.

The farmer straightened up and looked at him with smiling eyes. "Welcome to the kibbutz! Have you come a long way?"

Walter relaxed and smiled. *How simple it is to be welcoming*, he thought. "Maybe you can help me ..." he said hesitantly. "I've come from Tel Aviv. I'm looking for a woman who might live here."

The farmer looked warmly at him, and said, "Come, the dining room is closed already, you can dine with us, and stay overnight. Tomorrow morning I will go with you to the secretariat, where they can help you." Walter smiled and gladly accepted the offer. "And by the way, my name is Yankel." Walter was also quick to introduce himself.

Yankel placed in front of Walter a plate with a radish, a cucumber, and a coarsely cut tomato. Some green onions, a thick slice of bread, and a boiled egg. He passed Walter the salt shaker. "Eat. It's straight from the field. There is nothing better than that." They both ate, and after asking his guest, Yankel brought two cups of dark, sweet tea to the table. Walter raised the cup to his lips and was surprised to find mint leaves floating in it.

"There are countless ways to prepare tea," Walter said, filling his belly with the hot liquid. "The woman I am looking for served tea with lemon and a sugar cube, as she had learned from her father."

The farmer smiled at him.

"I'm afraid I won't find her here. I'm not looking forward to more disappointment." Walter added, "I heard a call on a radio show and thought there might be a chance she's on this kibbutz. I really hope I'm not wrong."

"Do not worry," Yankel said, "you'll find what your heart desires."

Walter smiled back at him.

**

The first rays of sun hit Walter's bed. The farmer was already dressed and ready for work. "Good morning!" he said loudly. "Get dressed, and I will show you where the secretariat is. Then I must go to the barn; the cows need to be milked."

Walter dressed quickly and walked with the man to the secretariat. "Good luck!" Yankel said and walked away.

Walter looked at the closed office door. A small sign indicated that the office would open after breakfast. He found his way to the dining room and sat down to eat a meal that rather resembled his dinner. He looked out over the green landscape through the window.

He ate quickly, almost inhaling the food, and rushed back

to the secretariat. Giora was waiting for him at the door. "Good morning," he said kindly. "How can I help you?"

"I heard some news about a Rivka on this kibbutz on the 'Search Bureau for Missing Relatives' radio program. Can you help me find that Rivka?"

"Of course! Come with me," Giora said. He led Walter to Rivka's door and went about his business.

Walter knocked on the door. Rivka was preparing to leave for work at the nursery. She would eat breakfast with the children. She was very surprised to see Walter at the door. She invited him in, and Walter entered with tentative steps. "I heard your message on the radio," he said. "I was hoping so much that it would be the same Rivka I met in Tel Aviv and fell desperately in love with." He came closer. "I lost my entire family too. I understand completely what you're going through."

Rivka remained still.

"Let me live by your side. We can give each other strength and comfort each other. There is no reason to be alone until you find them. No reason to be so lonely."

Rivka looked up at him.

"I promise when you find your family, I will leave you if that is your desire. In the meantime, why suffer alone when you can share your life with someone who loves you and wants you to hold on to life at any price? We must not lose hope that we will find them and be together again!"

At first, Rivka said nothing. After long minutes, she finally spoke. "I have to go to work now. You make a strong argument; let me think about it." She looked at him kindly, and before she walked through the door, he pulled her towards him and embraced her. She gave in to the hug, to the warmth she'd been missing so much. The idea that she should go through this period, waiting for a miracle, with a companion, had crossed her mind before. But she said nothing to encourage Walter. She walked off to the nursery, leaving him excited and hopeful.

At the end of the day, she stopped in Giora's office and shared with him what had happened earlier. "Don't worry. I'll help Walter to fit in here. We'll find him a job, and both of you can continue to search for your relatives," he said with a fatherly smile.

Within a few days, the couple moved in together. They left for work together in the mornings. She, to the nursery and he, to work at the office under Giora's supervision. Every evening, religiously, they listened to "Search Bureau for Missing Relatives." Every night, Walter comforted a disappointed Rivka. Despite their pain, their life became a blessed routine. Their nurturing of each other relieved their burdens and strengthened their friendship.

PART SIX: MENACHEM

Chapter 33

Northeast winds began to blow into New York from the frozen seas of Canada. The temperature, which dropped below zero, and the snow, froze Menachem's bones. Apart from some brief visits to Eastern Europe, he hadn't experienced this kind of cold in a while. Morocco, his homeland, had an abundance of sun and the land of Israel was also mostly warm. As he stood on the corner of 32nd Street and Fifth Avenue, briefcase in hand, he was buffeted by a wind so strong he felt he might fly from the curb into traffic. When the light changed, he ran, almost breathless, to his office and determined he'd better purchase some clothing that better suited this weather.

After work he went to visit Rachel at the post office. She smiled at him and motioned that she was just finishing up her shift. Menachem waited for her at the counter. She ran to him, wrapped her arm around his, and they left to grab a hot drink. Their daily life had become a very pleasant routine.

"Will you take me to a place where I can buy some warm clothes?" he asked with a smile. "I'm not used to this cold, and you are not with at all times to warm me up."

Rachel smiled and gladly agreed to help. Arm in arm, she walked with him to a menswear shop. She smiled at the salesman and rattled off a list of what Menachem needed: "He must have a sweater, a coat, and boots that are suitable for the winter." She enjoyed advising him and felt that with the shopping trip, her place beside him was becoming more secure. She showed that she was responsible and knowledgeable. In addition, her presence at his side let interested women know there was no point in flirting with him because he was taken. She couldn't have been happier.

To Rachel's great delight, Menachem invited her to his modest residence. In the middle of the night he briefly opened his eyes and saw Rivka. He needed a few minutes to calm his heartbeat and remember that Rachel was the one by his side. His heart was in tatters. He dreamt of Rivka and awoke to Rachel. The physical encounter with Rachel bore none of the passion he'd felt with Rivka. Suddenly, he felt alienated and distant from her.

In the morning, Rachel sat drinking tea, still hazy from the night, while Menachem quickly dressed in a suit and tie. Rachel felt uneasy, as if he were rushing her out of the house. But she said nothing.

As they went their separate ways for work, Rachel asked coyly, "Will you pick me up at the post office this evening?"

"Maybe. It depends on work."

Rachel cringed inside. She did not want to spend a

lonely evening in her own apartment. Being with Menachem warmed her soul.

Menachem did not come to the post office that night. Rachel's unease hardened into anxiety. She went home and waited. God knows for what. A sign.

That only came a week later. "I was away on a business trip," said Menachem with no details and no apology.

Menachem was conflicted as well. On the one hand, his loneliness was hard to bear, and when he wasn't with Rachel, he longed for her. But when he was with her, he felt a nagging disappointment. Through no fault of her own, Rachel simply wasn't Rivka.

The uncertainty about when she'd see him again ate at Rachel; she felt like a neglected child. And she behaved so when she was finally with him. She was miserable. Eating became increasingly difficult, and often she vomited right after a meal. Physical weakness and extreme fatigue dragged her down. She functioned as well as she could at work, but collapsed when she returned to her empty home and the demons there. There were many nights when she just lay in bed crying. Her menstrual cycle stopped, and she felt that her body was collapsing.

Chapter 34

Rachel pulled herself out of bed and dressed reluctantly for work. In the past she had chosen her dresses carefully, putting on lipstick and matching colors. She enjoyed feeling feminine, and it pleased her when men who came to her counter peeped at her and admired her looks. Now, however, because she knew she wouldn't see Menachem, she pulled clothes off the shelf carelessly, with no regard for how they looked.

She sat down reluctantly at her desk, waiting for the day to be over, barely working. Fatigue, lack of desire, and depression were present in her every movement and gesture. Mina, her friend, approached her. "Maybe you need a break," she suggested, and with a sly smile she glanced pointedly at Rachel's belly.

Rachel did not understand the meaning of the smile.

"Maybe you got married and didn't tell me?" Mina continued.

Rachel turned pale. How had she not thought about that? She'd noticed that she'd put on some weight, but she attributed it to her general unhealthy state and her tendency to overindulge in sweets when she was upset. Panic took over. Cold sweat beaded on her forehead. Her heart pounded. Her brain was moving quickly. She didn't know where Menachem was or how to contact him. A quick calculation confirmed that she might be in the third or fourth month of her pregnancy.

"Yes, thank you, that's a good idea," said Rachel, swallowing the pool of saliva that had collected in her mouth. She put up the sign indicating that her counter was closed. She pushed her chair from the desk and began to walk away, but her legs failed. Mina grabbed her before she fell, and guided her out into the open air.

"Is the father the man who used to pick you up from work? Why haven't we seen him around lately?" Mina asked.

Rachel burst into tears. The depths of her despair and depression, the melancholy and the anguish that she had borne stoically over the recent months, emerged unbidden. Her tears streamed uncontrollably.

"I can't believe this," she cried. "I just cannot believe this." The knowledge that she was pregnant made her feel trapped in the prison that her life had become. "What am I supposed to do about this now?"

Mina wiped her friend's eyes and her nose with a handkerchief from her pocket. She hugged Rachel and gave her a shoulder to cry on.

"How am I supposed to raise another creature in this world, when I can barely keep myself on my feet?"

"Everything will be just fine," Mina reassured her. "You will stay with us. You will not have to cook or clean. You will have your own room, and you will not have to pay rent."

Rachel looked up at Mina, and for the first time her cries subsided a little.

"And when the child is born, we will help you feed him and take care of him. You're not alone!" Mina said excitedly.

"Thank you, Mina. That's so generous of you, but I can't interfere with your life. I would be a burden on you and your husband. A young couple like you needs your privacy."

"If Dan himself invites you, will it ease your mind?" Mina asked. "You'll see, he will be so excited." Mina was in her thirties and had been married to Dan for several years. Despite numerous attempts, they weren't able to have a baby. The unexpected pregnancy of Rachel moved Mina indescribably.

The postmaster was also in favor of the proposal. Dan was hesitant at first, but after a lengthy conversation with his wife he extended an invitation to Rachel to come and live with them. "Having you around will bring us happiness and a baby in the house will thrill us even more," he told Rachel. She was at last convinced.

In the morning Rachel and Mina took the subway to work together. And in the evening they returned home together. It's impossible to describe Rachel's relief at being able to go through each day with Mina's assistance and to return to a home full of life instead of an empty apartment. Her anxiety over the pregnancy and the burden of raising a child was replaced by the pleasure of living together. Rachel helped as much as she could with light housework and began to look forward to the birth.

She tried to get out of the house in the evenings occasionally, when she wasn't exhausted, to give Mina and Dan some time to themselves that they were surely lacking. She didn't pay any attention to their whispered conversations.

Chapter 35

Menachem returned to New York. He'd missed the pulse of the city while he'd been away on business and was glad to be back for some meetings. Being home made him miss Rivka, and the loneliness made him miss Rachel. He decided to visit her at the post office before his first appointment.

He looked around the post office lobby and couldn't find her. He thought she might be on vacation or home sick. Just to be sure, however, he went to the manager and asked about her. He was shocked to hear that Rachel was at the hospital — in the maternity ward. How was it possible that he did not know anything about it? He didn't remember seeing any indication that she was pregnant when he saw her last.

He thanked the manager for the news and wandered out of the building. As he meandered down the sidewalk, he traveled nine months back in his mind. *How long since I've seen her?* He calculated. Suddenly he realized: He'd been gone from New York for nine months. One mission was followed by another, and task followed task. If you'd asked, he would have said he'd been gone only four months, six at the most. Instead, nine months had passed and that meant the newborn was likely his offspring! He momentarily stiffened and froze, not knowing what to do. He'd been walking around mechanically and had stepped into the street without looking first. His stomach turned. A car horn woke him from his reverie and he leapt back to the sidewalk.

He decided to go to the hospital that the manager had named. A short chat at the information desk led to him to Rachel. In the elevator, a man and a woman whispered to each other in Polish. Hearing the language, which he knew from his trips to Europe, Menachem's ears sharpened. The couple would not have suspected that the American-looking man in the business suit understood their language.

The man, in his late thirties, gave the woman, who looked like his mother, some instructions. "You'll take the baby from the hospital and bring it to your house."

The woman looked at him with complete concentration, like a loyal soldier.

"Mina will tell her that the baby died, and slowly we'll push Rachel out of the house." He stopped to see if she was following. "After she leaves, we can take the baby back from you." The man finished speaking and gave the woman an encouraging smile. She remained so serious that it wasn't clear how much she understood.

The hair on the back of Menachem's neck stood up and his flesh tingled. He had a bad feeling. There were too many coincidences. Why, out of all names in the world, were they whispering about a Rachel? He was quick to exit and hurry down the hall to the maternity ward.

Chapter 36

Menachem's instinct guided him this time around as well. In an instant he became a wild animal. His senses sharpened, his heart was pounding, and he acted intuitively. He called the hospital security officer and two of his coworkers. He wasn't sure that this was indeed his Rachel, but whoever this Rachel was, she did not deserve someone kidnapping her baby and going through life believing that her baby had died. He told the security officer to stand outside the delivery room and keep an eye on visitors who seemed suspicious. He described in detail the couple in the elevator and the woman in particular. Then he turned to the nursing staff.

"Who here knows Rachel? A new mother with blue eyes and light flowing hair? There are little freckles on her nose."

One of the nurses looked up. "I am in charge of her delivery, may I help you, sir?" *So, it is my Rachel!*

After explaining, short of breath, what he heard in the elevator, he asked the nurse to stay with the mother at all times. He described Rachel to her again to make sure there would be no mistakes. "I have another small request," he said as walked with her towards the delivery room. "Can you please tell her that Menachem is out here, waiting for her and the baby?"

The nurse flashed him an understanding smile and entered Rachel's room with a glass of water.

Menachem went back to the security officer. In the meantime, his friends from the embassy arrived. He pointed discreetly at the approaching couple. Mina wore the same smile she always had for her friend. She walked into the delivery room to hold Rachel's hand.

Rachel, who was already in the delivery process, screamed and gripped Mina's hand with every exhale and push. Meanwhile, plainclothes police officers were spread throughout the building. They posed as regular visitors, standing around and occasionally glancing at random, imperceptibly, at the events around Rachel's room.

The baby boy was placed in Rachel's arms. "Hello, welcome," she said, very tired. Shortly, the baby was taken from her to be weighed, wiped, and diapered. When the nurse brought him back, Mina asked to hold him. Rachel agreed with a weary smile. She closed her eyes briefly.

Mina, holding the baby, very excited, was about to walk out to give him to Dan's mother. As soon as she crossed the threshold, the undercover cops surrounded her. "I'll take that, thank you very much," Menachem said and took the newborn in his hands gently.

Mina couldn't breathe. She watched her dream of a baby

drifting away. Her eyes were streaming with tears, not because of the handcuffs or the words of the policemen — she was unaware of those — but because they had stolen her baby from her! She cried out and fell to the floor. The policemen grabbed her by the arms and led her to the squad car. Dan and his elderly mother were already in the car, handcuffed and in shock as well. A nurse who had been bribed with a lot of money was arrested later.

Menachem walked gently, holding the small package that was his son, smiling at him, and approached a fatigued Rachel. She was oblivious to the commotion that had just happened. He kissed her on the forehead. "We have a lovely son," he said. She burst into tears of relief and happiness. "I'm glad I arrived in time for the birth. Traveling from Israel to New York is not a small matter." He smiled at her and stroked her head. "From now on we won't be apart anymore," he assured her.

The next morning, Menachem visited the hospital with a bouquet of flowers. He put it in a vase next to Rachel, who was sitting up in bed, feeding their son. He was overcome with elation about this child after so many solitary years devoted to his work for the new Jewish nation.

"How are you this morning?" he asked with a smile.

Rachel smiled at him, not yet recovered from the birth.

He asked to hold his son.

She set the baby tenderly in Menachem's outstretched arms.

"Do you know what we should call him yet?" he asked.

"I have some ideas," she replied with a smile.

"You know, we're lucky." She looked up at him. "The couple you lived with were not the friends you thought they were."

With a furrowed brow she asked, "What do you mean?"

"When I got to the hospital, I heard them going over a detailed plan of how they would kidnap our son and give him to Dan's mother until they could get rid of you. They also planned to tell you that the baby died."

Horror and disbelief spread over Rachel's tired face. "No, it's not possible. They took me into their home! They took care of me. They couldn't have been involved in such a horrible plot!" Rachel held out her hands for her son. She had an immediate and urgent need to hold him again. To protect him. The thought she might have lost him made her tremble.

Suddenly, the snippets of conversations she had heard in Mina's apartment started to make sense. Mina and her husband sometimes conversed in Polish. After all, they weren't aware that she understood the language, and so spoke it freely around her. Like her mother before her, some innate survival instinct had encouraged her to hide her native language in America and only use it as a secret language.

She recalled talks about her stay, conversations with Dan's mother, everything connected to the awful scenario that Menachem explained to her. At once, the puzzle was solved, and she knew that Menachem told the truth. They had taken advantage of her being in need, innocent, and alone. She realized that this was the reason they had invited her to live with them from the start.

Again, she burst into tears. This time, tears of relief. She hugged her baby and Menachem firmly, convinced that her hardship was over and that she had finally reached a state of happiness.

Chapter 37

To his small bachelor apartment, which came with his posting to New York, Menachem brought Rachel and the baby. He took care of all their needs, and she took care of the apartment and her two men, as she called them. They decided to name their son Jacob after Rachel's father.

They combined their wedding festivities with their son's bris. Menachem's colleagues held a reception in their honor — a few refreshments and a lot of smiles.

The postmaster served as the witness on Rachel's side. She was one of his best employees, and he was very fond of her. He was amazed at their story and the rescue operation at the hospital. He couldn't believe that Mina was capable of such a malicious plan.

"I learned about it from an article in the newspaper that reported the circumstances of her arrest along with Dan and his mother and gave information about the coming trial," he said and sighed about their evil souls and probably about all the evil in the world.

At the end of the wedding ceremony they conducted the bris. A friend of Menachem's from work held Jacob on a soft white pillow. The baby rested peacefully through the circumcision. The *mohel* encouraged everybody to celebrate with a dance, but Rachel just wanted everything to be over so she could feed Jacob in the back room.

They brought Jacob to her, and the rabbi showed her how to treat the wound. She was a little nervous, so the next day, the rabbi came and helped her bathe Jacob. He brought a few pacifiers made of cloth and dipped in grape juice. Jacob took to the pacifier with gusto. Until then, he'd refused pacifiers and was glued to Rachel's breast. She was so glad that it could give her some rest from feeding, that she asked the rabbi if he had any more pacifiers and also how to make them. They finished bathing him, applied some ointment, and the rabbi blessed them both before leaving.

Menachem went back to his job. He kept his trips as short as possible and helped Rachel with the baby as much as he could.

Jacob grew and began to murmur a little lying on his stomach, attempting his first crawls. Rachel was always very tired when Menachem came home, and he saw that they needed his help.

"What do you think about making an aliyah to Israel?" he asked one evening. "I can talk with my sister, Leah. She can help us find a nice apartment on the kibbutz and could also help us with Jacob."

A broad smile spread across Rachel's face. She had been longing for some help, but there was no one to ask. Actually, she was quite lonely in New York, and the bitterness of what had happened there still lingered, encouraging her to jump on the offer. It seemed like the right move.

"Great idea! I can't wait to go." She smiled at Menachem and even little Jacob joined in, cooing and smiling.

They began packing and dealing with the bureaucracies involved in such a move and purchased their tickets. Their ship was scheduled to dock on the coast of Israel at beginning of the year, during the early holidays.

Chapter 38

Rachel felt ill. She leaned over the rail and vomited mightily. She was hoping that the fresh air on deck would do her good. After several minutes she straightened up, but as soon as she looked out over the water she immediately bent over the railing again. Her stomach was empty and only bile was left in it. She was thankful that Menachem was used to these journeys and unbothered by seasickness, and so could watch over the baby, who was sleeping peacefully. For Jacob, the rocking of the boat was actually pleasant and reminded him of his mother's womb.

She returned to their cabin and Menachem looked up to see her entering, exhausted and pale. The nausea didn't relent for the entire long trip. Her mood was very fragile, and she felt weak all the time. It was very hard for her to take care of Jacob. Menachem helped her as much as he could and was as eager as his wife to walk on land again.

Leah was waiting for them anxiously. She and Menachem were very close; his inability to attend her wedding had intensified her yearning to see him once more. Ever since she had learned that he had a child, her longing to see him and his new family had grown even stronger.

She had prepared a modest one-bedroom apartment for them on the kibbutz, taken care of furnishings, and cleaned it with her friends a little each day. She painted it white and hung some cheerful green curtains. Her eagerness to see him motivated her to work on the apartment in her spare time. She got some basic kitchen utensils, ones that were also suitable for preparing baby food. She got bedding and towels, and placed scented soaps in the closets that were waiting to be filled up with their clothes.

The cleaning tools — the broom and the mop — she put in a small utility closet, and when she shut the door behind her, everything was ready for their arrival. They would not have to lift a finger. Her wish was that when they arrived after the arduous journey, they would be able to rest and acclimate quickly to the country.

The day of docking in Israel finally arrived. Leah checked to make sure that the ship had not been delayed and asked Giora to bring them back with him on his way home from Tel Aviv. He would be in the city for the monthly meeting of the kibbutz secretaries and to buy some equipment needed for the kibbutz. He gladly agreed. It was part of his job as secretary to welcome new members of the kibbutz, whether they were single volunteers or families who came to settle.

The ship docked, and people began to flow slowly down the

gangplank. Menachem and Rachel, Jacob and suitcase, found themselves wondering which way to turn. Suddenly they saw Giora. Menachem recognized him and was very glad to see a friendly face. Giora greeted them with warm hugs and led them to his truck. He took the suitcase from Menachem so he could help Rachel, who was still very weak. They had brought the few possessions they had accumulated in New York, believing they would find all they needed on the kibbutz.

They crammed into the cab of the truck, and put the suitcase in the truck bed, where the new tools that Giora had bought were rattling around. Menachem held little Jacob on his lap. Rachel felt as bad on the road as she had on the ocean. The shaking and fatigue got the better of her, and she asked to stop several times. By nightfall they finally arrived at the kibbutz. Giora led them all the way to their door, where Leah waited for them.

Leah fell into her brother's arms and immediately turned to the little crown prince with words of affection. She hugged Rachel and said, "I see that you deserve congratulations."

"Yes, thank you," Rachel replied thinking that Leah was congratulating her on the wedding and the birth of her son. When she saw that Leah was looking at her stomach, she suddenly realized she was pregnant again. Rachel found it difficult to handle all the emotional stress and rushed into her new home. Leah's touch was evident in every corner of the house and the loving attention calmed Rachel. A new and refreshing smell greeted her, an Israeli scent. She smiled. The breeze of change was welcome.

Chapter 39

Rachel got up the next morning with a smile on her face. Menachem had let her sleep in, and he'd taken Jacob for a walk to familiarize himself with the kibbutz. She sat up in bed and saw a spot of blood on her clothes. A scream startled the neighbors, "ME-NA-CH-EM!" Tears came to her eyes. It was only the day before that she realized she was pregnant and now the baby might be in trouble.

Menachem arrived within minutes. He saw the bloodstain, and his delight over the second child was replaced by fear. "Don't worry, I'm going to call a doctor," he said while trying to calm himself as well. He instinctively ordered her, "Stay in bed and don't move. I'll be right back!"

The doctor determined that the journey had been too tough on her. First, the turmoil of the ship and then the journey by truck over rough roads. Rachel was confined to bed rest. He forbade her to pick up her son and advised the couple to give him to the kibbutz's day care to make things easier for them.

Leah came the next morning to take her nephew to day care and introduce him to the teachers and the other little kibbutz members. She asked the teacher to try and spoil him more than usual in the first few days since he had never been away from his mother before.

"His mother," she told the teacher, "is on strict bed rest and the doctor has instructed her not to get out of bed or to engage in any physical activity. And right now little Jacob wants to crawl and explore the world; physical activity in the nursery is exactly what he needs."

Rivka, the teacher, lifted Jacob up, smiled at him, and he smiled back at her.

"Don't worry, he'll have a lot of fun here," she reassured Leah.

The hours in the day care center with the children were the most beautiful hours of the day for Rivka. The little children made her happy, and she temporarily forgot the hardships that weighed on her. She was at ease in the company of innocents who knew only goodness and love.

Chapter 40

Menachem spent his evenings taking care of Jacob. Bath, play, and dinner. Rachel was served her supper in bed.

"Maybe I can get up to help you?" she asked him.

"Absolutely not!" He did not want to take even the smallest of risks that something might happen to his wife or unborn child.

They slowly adapted to life on the kibbutz. Menachem even brought Rachel outdoors in a wheelchair to take in a little sunshine. The bright sunlight had a good effect on their mood, and they were in a kind of blissful tranquility. They found that routine gave them a new kind of freedom.

The message that Menachem had to return to New York destabilized their lives. Such a trip meant he would be absent for months. Menachem knew that Rachel could not manage alone, so he asked Leah to help her in his stead. She would need to take Jacob to and from day care and be with them in the afternoons until Jacob fell asleep. In the mornings, she would have to go first to the apartment, prepare food for

Rachel, and dress Jacob. And of course she'd need to be there on the weekend.

"Don't worry about a thing, Menachem, it's the least I can do for you. Go in peace, dear brother," Leah said. Menachem was able to relax and prepare for his upcoming travels.

Leah, who was not used to interrupting her routine to pick Jacob up at exactly 3:30, had a little trouble with the new schedule. She wasn't managing her work very well. Sometimes she needed to steal a few extra minutes to complete one task or another. On one of those occasions, she was late leaving to pick Jacob up from day care and didn't notice that it was already past four o'clock. She panicked when she looked at her watch — half past four. She ran to the day care center, but there was no one there. Leah guessed that Rivka must have taken Jacob to her home when no one had come to pick him up and headed for Rivka's house.

Rivka was happy in Jacob's company. Having him around allowed her to extend the hours that she enjoyed the most. They played in her yard, and indoors, she encouraged him as he took his first steps supported by pieces of furniture.

Walter was delighted at the sight of Rivka full of laughter. It had been a long time since he'd seen her that way at home. It seemed to him that she left her good cheer behind the walls of the nursery. He wanted so much to see such gaiety in their home. He decided to find out if it would be possible for Rivka to spend time with Jacob on a regular basis after hours. He asked Leah when she came to pick up Jacob. She promised to find out from her sister-in-law but suggested to him that it would probably not be a problem.

Rachel accepted the offer gladly. It eased her mind to know Jacob would be cared for and entertained and that Leah wouldn't be as burdened. Her second pregnancy was much harder on her than the first, and she was still confined to bed.

Rivka grew attached to Jacob with every fiber of her soul. He had given her back the will to live. Every night she waited impatiently for the next morning when she would see him again at the day care center. At the end of the day, Leah picked Jacob up from Rivka's house and brought him home to his mother. Rachel was pleased that her child was well cared for, happy, and smiling. She attributed it to the company of other toddlers and the tender treatment he received.

Rachel wrote Menachem a letter telling him about the wonderful teacher who was helping her and Leah with Jacob. And about how the arrangement cheered her. He decided to return to Israel with a gift for the teacher who nurtured his son so affectionately.

On his way home, a woman was in the window of a jewelry store near his office changing the display. A delicate silver bracelet caught his eye. The links of the chain were woven together like tiny ships one after another with finesse, and in the center was an oval coin. On the coin were the raised image of a palm tree and a figure dressed in a Roman toga, wearing a wreath of olive leaves. He decided to buy the same bracelet for the teacher, for his sister, and for his dear wife.

When he next set sail for the long journey to Israel, he kept the bracelets close to his heart, in the pocket of his shirt.

Chapter 41

The ship docked in Israel, and Menachem traveled by bus to the north. He arrived home excited, eager to see his wife and son. When he went in the apartment, Jacob was already asleep. He found Rachel also in bed: on her side, surrounded by pillows on every side — a pillow under her stomach, a pillow between her knees, a pillow behind her back, and a pillow under her arm. It was the only way she could fall asleep. The long months of lying in bed and only getting up for the bathroom had weakened her. Her sleep was very light.

Menachem closed the bedroom door softly, but she awoke anyway. She could not resist getting up to hug him. The sudden excitement and motion brought on labor instantly. She nearly collapsed from the intense pain. Menachem, excited, rushed her to the hospital with the generous help of Giora in the kibbutz van, but not before he'd summoned Leah to look after Jacob.

Rachel spent long hours in the maternity room, struggling through the intense contractions. In the early morning, their second son came into the world. His eyes, when they opened, were blue, like his mother's. Menachem and Rachel hugged their son. The tiny creature filled them with new spirit and banished the difficulty of the recent months. They cried uncontrollably, but only with relief and elation.

Rachel was in pain, but she was glad that she could finally walk around again. She took advantage of the days in the hospital by accepting the assistance of the nurses, giving her hours of needed rest before returning home.

Giora helped to organize an impressive bris celebration for their new son. The dining room was decorated, and the best crops of the season made their way into tasty, appetizing dishes. Colorful fresh salads, hard and soft cheeses, fresh-baked pastries and sweet desserts.

Rachel and Menachem stood at the entrance to the hall welcoming the guests, the newborn in Rachel's arms and Menachem holding Jacob by the hand. Without warning, Jacob broke away and ran towards a light-haired woman who had just entered. She hugged him close to her, and he was clearly very happy to see her. "This must be his teacher," Rachel whispered in Menachem's ear as they went over to meet her. Rivka stood up, smiled in their direction and froze.

Shock spread over Rachel's face: She couldn't believe what she was seeing. It was her mother! Rivka! Her mother was the one who took such loving care of her son. Rivka was astounded to discover that Jacob, the charming boy she'd fallen desperately in love with, was her grandson. Her daughter had not been lost to her after all. She instantly understood that he was called Jacob after his grandfather — her husband. The happiness and astonishment were tempered by a jolt that left her speechless when she realized she already knew her daughter's husband: It was Menachem. His response was very much the same, as a shudder ran through his whole body.

Long minutes, so it seemed, they stood stunned. Rachel was the first to recover, and she fell onto her mother's neck and hugged her tightly. She was elated to discover that her mother was alive. Rachel's hug melted Rivka's paralysis, and she smiled at her daughter and gazed at Jacob again.

"My Rakhel, Rakhel, Rakhel, Rakhel," she murmured incessantly as she hugged her daughter.

"Rakhel!" Menachem said, trying to recover from the impact of coming face to face with the woman who embraced his wife. "It is indeed a more appropriate name here, in the Holy Land."

She smiled at him and said, "Yes, that is the name I was given. Menachem, this is my mother, Rivka."

Rivka and Menachem looked at each other and didn't know what to do with themselves.

"Nice to meet you," he blurted.

Rivka smiled, horribly embarrassed, and quickly turned her gaze back to Rachel. She decided to focus on the good news. This is what she had been living for, to find her children again, was it not? Her legs still weak from shock, Rivka moved with difficulty. Rachel and Rivka, holding each other up, turned towards the hall. Everyone cheered the happy reunion along with the celebration of the bris. Walter invited the whole family to their home to catch up. He was so happy that Rivka's daughter had been found and was relieved that Rivka's husband was not there.

Chapter 42

Menachem tossed and turned all night. He tried to do so gently so as not to disturb Rachel, who slept very lightly and awoke at every little cry or sigh from the baby. Rachel could not sleep because of her husband's insomnia but said nothing. She assumed he had difficulty falling asleep due to the great excitement of the family reunification.

Rivka also tossed and turned in her bed. Walter slept deeply, while she tried to digest the events of the day over and over again. She couldn't stop thinking about the surprising encounter. She looked forward to the following day when she could continue talking with her daughter and find out what had happened to her since they parted from each other. The next day, Rivka, instead of waiting for him to be picked up, brought Jacob directly to Rachel and Menachem's home. Walter joined them there.

Rivka, settling in to her new role as a grandmother, approached the new baby and picked him up. She hugged him, patted his back, and whispered soothing words in his ear.

"Sweet David," she whispered. Her eyes opened wide and she shivered as she suddenly realized something. "My David. You called him David because of him?" she asked Rachel.

"Yes, Mom. David ..."

Rivka looked again at little David. "You'll be for me as my little David that is no more," she said, her eyes filling with moisture.

Menachem was pacing like a caged lion. He brought tea and cookies for everyone, hoping that keeping busy would help ease his restlessness. "Excuse me, ladies," he said to Rachel and Rivka, "I'll leave you two alone. You've got a lot of catching up to do."

Each one gave him her most melting smile, and he went out to the balcony for a cigarette. Walter joined him and they smoked in silence. *So lucky*, he thought, *that men do not feel the need to talk much.*

After a few long minutes, just to be polite, Walter said, "These are exciting times."

"Yes," Menachem sighed. He did not know if he would have preferred not to have this thrill that also introduced a new complication in his life, but at the same time, he was truly happy. "A mother found her daughter," he muttered. "This is a blessing."

Rivka and Rachel could not stop talking. They wanted to cram years into hours. Rachel told her mother about the carpentry shop her father had opened. "The shop prospered right away," she said, "and later he joined Uncle Icho's huge construction company that he had started with some friends from Poland. He was doing really well, but then Aunt Hannah and her entire family perished in a car accident."

Rivka gasped.

"From there everything started to deteriorate. Dad was not able to function both as provider and a single parent. David felt abandoned, neglected, like nobody understands him, I'm guessing. I tried, Mom. I really tried to be there for him. But the boys were in boarding school. It was out of my hands." Rachel lowered her head sadly. "From that moment, it was a steep slope down. David's suicide sent Dad into the bottle, and he died of cirrhosis of the liver." A heavy burden rested on Rachel. She glanced over at little David and Jacob asleep in bed. Her love for them gave her strength to continue. "Laibel was also strongly affected by David's death. He chose to break away from us and lock himself in a boarding school in Brooklyn. He only finds comfort in religion now."

Rivka rested a comforting hand on her daughter's back. "Not everything is in our control. I know you did your best for the family. When you hear what happened on this side of the world, you'll realize that even though your mother also did her best, I didn't always achieve the desired results."

Rivka told her daughter about the horrible day the Germans killed her father, her mother, and most of the Jewish residents of Nadvorna. She told Rachel how she'd been spared after she had fainted, and perhaps only because she had fainted. How David's dog saved her. How she ran away with Rex from Max.

How she joined the partisans and how she came to Israel.

"And here, I was assigned to be a translator in an office in Tel Aviv, but I couldn't find peace and I was lonely," she said and glanced towards the balcony. "My best friend, Bilhah, arranged a home for me on the kibbutz and I've been here ever since."

They both sipped their cups of hot tea with lemon that reminded them of home. Walter and Menachem came in from the balcony leaving the cold night breeze behind. "Rivka darling, I hope you don't mind, but I'm going home now. Take your time and just get there when you get there."

Rivka smiled at him and nodded gratefully. She was grateful for the respectful partnership they had built over the years. Menachem accompanied Walter home and enjoyed the refreshing walk at that late hour. Once they left the apartment the women were again on their own with only the snoring babies for company.

Rivka had been putting off asking her daughter where and how she'd met her husband. She did not even mention the name Menachem, and harsh stomach tremors attacked her when Rachel began the story of how they met. "One day, a handsome man came to the post office where I worked to send a wedding present to his sister on the kibbutz. There was a special moment there, when I think I can say I fell in love. He started courting me and came to the post office every day."

Rivka tried to appear calm and celebrate her daughter's good fortune, but the cramps in her belly had become more and more intense. "Excuse me please," Rivka requested and ran to the bathroom to throw up.

She looked in the mirror as she washed her face and rinsed out her mouth. *How long have I lived on the kibbutz? she wondered. And all this time I've been living next to my beloved's sister. Well, how could I have known when I keep everything a secret?* She splashed a little more water on her face, collected herself, and went back to Rachel.

"Are you feeling well, Mother?" Rachel asked with an anxious expression.

"Yes, yes. Please, continue your story." Rivka sat down and took a deep breath.

"Well," said Rachel and a slight crease appeared between her eyebrows, "not everything was smooth. There was a time when we separated and didn't see each other for many months. That was when I discovered my first pregnancy. A colleague invited me to stay with her and her husband. I thought it was out of the kindness of her heart, however, it turned out to be a sinister plot to kidnap my Jacob and tell me that he had died at birth."

Rivka was appalled. "And how was it resolved?"

"Thanks to Menachem. He came back to New York in time, like a divine calling, and learned that I was about to give birth. In the hospital, he heard a conversation in Polish, the plot of my friend and her husband. He was the one who saved us. And from then on, we have been inseparable. We combined our wedding with Jacob's bris and a few months after he was born, we decided to move to Israel. And here we are. The hand of fate directed us to the same kibbutz you were living in, Mom! And to top it all off, it was also the same kibbutz that Menachem's sister lives in!"

They hugged for a long while. Little David began to cry, and Rachel got up to feed him. She looked out the window, and saw it was already dawn. *Where is Menachem?* she thought. She looked over and saw him asleep in bed. How did she not notice that he had returned? She went back to her mother carrying David wrapped up in a blanket. Relaxed and sleepy. They embraced again. Rivka stood up and stretched muscles stiff from the long night sitting on the couch.

"My dear daughter, I am so happy to see you again. The only thing that kept me going through all the many trials was the hope that I would see my children again. Now I will go get a little rest before the workday starts, and we will meet again tomorrow."

The two parted with hugs and kisses. Rivka returned to her apartment, where Walter was waiting. He was awake and sleepless from the exciting encounter. He was happy for Rivka and couldn't wait to hear the details. She told him about Menachem's work in New York and his many trips overseas, and how when he returned from one of them, he discovered that Rachel was pregnant, and not only that, but he foiled an evil plot to kidnap little Jacob. She told him everything in detail, except her one secret. Walter listened patiently and suddenly a mischievous look sparkled in his eyes.

"I have an idea. Tell me how you feel about it. What do you think about traveling to New York with Menachem on his next trip? You can try to find Laibel, all alone in a foreign land. You can meet him and try to persuade him to move to the land of Israel."

Rivka froze. She was scared of how she would handle her feelings when she was alone with Menachem. After a long pause she said, "It's an interesting idea. It's just that this hit me all at once. It's all so confusing, but I promise to think about it." She kissed Walter good night and covered herself with a blanket as if to disappear entirely.

PART SEVEN: RIVKA AND MENACHEM

Chapter 43

Menachem was not able to find any rest. This wasn't how he wished to find his beloved Rivka. He could not touch her, could not show her that he still loved her and how terrible it was — she was the mother of his wife. His beloved, the one he really wanted was his children's grandmother. He felt trapped. And on the other hand, there were his two children, and Rachel resembled her mother so much. He was also a man of his word, and his promise to Rachel still stood. His relations with both brought on a sense of sin and incest. All of this must be kept secret and not shared with Rachel, and if he wanted to talk to Rivka, it would add insult to injury and a secret on top of a secret. How could he continue to live like this? His tortured soul found no solution or rest, and at night he tossed and turned, sometimes until dawn.

He could not allow himself to run into Rivka, and he did all he could to avoid any encounters with her, no matter how innocent. He knew that he had to get out of this situation but did not know how.

He received a call from work and was offered the opportunity to lead the instruction of new agents in Tel Aviv. Suddenly, a resolution emerged. He was relieved a little, and as it says in the Book of Esther: "relief and deliverance will rise for the Jews from another place." But at night, when he put his two innocent children to bed, doubt caught up with him again. "Rakhelinka," he said after he left the boys' room, "I've been selected to lead the training of the new agents in Tel Aviv. I'm contemplating whether to move to the center of the country or to travel every morning and come back to bed at night here with you on the kibbutz."

Rachel thought briefly about it. "Perhaps there is a compromise?" She looked at him with empathy. "Maybe you can rent an apartment and come on weekends to be with us? I will have enough help here, with Leah and my mother; we'll manage." And she smiled at him.

He smiled with relief and hugged her. She could not know what else was on his mind and was unaware of the greater distress he dealt with. And even if she did notice, she didn't always see fit to investigate.

Rachel was so happy to be reunited with her mother. Rivka had missed so much all those years and now was back, exactly when she was most needed. The children and her mother filled Rachel's whole world. She felt that she could release Menachem a little from her strong dependence on him.

Menachem was happy and relieved. He rented a small room in Tel Aviv and every Thursday evening returned to the kibbutz for Friday dinner with his family and a stroll in nature on Saturday. He did everything he could, even on the weekends, to avoid the slightest of interactions with Rivka.

Rachel was very fond of Walter, especially in light of Rivka's stories about how he had comforted her and how, when she moved to the kibbutz, leaving no address, he looked for her. Rivka told her how much he had helped her during their separation — the hope he gave her as they listened to "Search Bureau for Missing Relatives" and how he encouraged her when she was disappointed time and time again that there was no answer to her request.

One day, Rachel arrived at Rivka's home, carrying David, to pick Jacob up. Walter opened the door.

"Come on in. Rivka and Jacob are probably delayed because they are smelling the flowers on their way home."

She smiled and went inside.

Walter poured her a glass of cold water. "Here you go, drink."

Rachel took a small sip and put the glass on the counter. She walked around lightly, rocking a little, so David would continue sleeping.

"You know, Rivka is so much happier since she discovered that her daughter and grandsons live so close by!"

Rachel smiled.

"I had an idea I wanted to share with you, to complete the family."

Rachel gave him a questioning look but said nothing so she

didn't disturb David's sleep.

"Well," Walter continued, "Laibel, your brother, is still in New York, in the boarding school, is that right?"

Rachel nodded.

"What do you think about Rivka joining Menachem on his upcoming trip to New York to find him? It would be difficult for her alone, but Menachem can do it more easily. All he has to do is grow a beard and wear a yarmulke. That way he could gain Laibel's trust, and reintroduce him to his mother. Rivka will have to persuade him to return with her to Israel."

"It's not a bad idea!" she whispered.

"He won't be able to refuse to reunite with his family after he hears how happy you are to be together again," Walter said.

And so, Walter talked to Rivka, and Rachel talked to Menachem. Slowly the idea started to come together in their minds. Rivka really wanted to see her son, Laibel, but she feared what might happen when she was alone with Menachem. Because of that concern, she let the matter drop and didn't pursue any more conversations on the subject.

Rachel decided to take the reins. She very much missed the one brother she had left. She would be very happy to have him there with the whole family.

She invited Walter and her mother for dinner. When Menachem came home, she told him that she was throwing a festive Shabbat dinner. The table was full of tasty dishes. The kids were in bed when the four of them sat down to eat. Rivka complimented her daughter on the delicious food.

"I recognize this recipe," Rivka said with a smile. "I miss Grandma Masha so much."

Walter and Rachel just talked and talked and didn't feel the tension between Rivka and Menachem. Those two listened in silence most of the time. Occasionally one of them mumbled a word of agreement. The plan began to take shape.

"Before we do anything, I must finish the course I supervise in Tel Aviv," said Menachem, and they all agreed that the trip would take place after the end of his assignment.

Chapter 44

The monthly meeting of the kibbutz secretaries in Tel Aviv, which Giora attended, coincided with Rivka and Menachem's departure. Giora invited them to join him on the road trip and offered to drive them to the Port of Jaffa.

Rivka and Menachem loaded their luggage into the kibbutz truck. Rivka wrapped herself tightly in her shawl to protect herself from the morning chill. They left at dawn. Rivka tried not to even glance at Menachem without a reason. She was determined to carry on with her life, no matter what, and focus on the godsend of the family reunion.

Giora sat in the driver's seat and Rivka and Menachem squeezed into the cab with him. The bumps along the road made their knees touch from time to time. Rivka tried to concentrate on the road ahead and breathe. She looked out the window, watching the trees. Her eyes envisioned a string that connected one treetop to another, each electrical pole to the next. The sun was rising on the horizon, and she began to warm up.

It was afternoon when they arrived at the port. Menachem picked up both of their bags. Rivka found her cabin, unpacked her clothes, and put them in the dresser. When she finished, she walked out on deck determined to avoid Menachem.

Menachem, who was so used to traveling, simply put his suitcase under the bed and lay down. He stared at the ceiling. When he heard Rivka's footsteps returning to her cabin, he walked out to the deck. He made every effort to avoid meeting her unnecessarily. The few times they did meet, they talked only about their plan to find Laibel and went their separate ways.

At night, when the waves rocked them, Menachem wrapped himself in his blanket, stared at the ceiling, and felt Rivka's presence even through the walls. All his being called out for her. He saw images from their days together in Europe. His hands were burning with longing to touch her body. Tastes, smells, and feelings came back. He swallowed his saliva and turned on his side, as if trying to find other thoughts that might be on the other side of his bed.

He found no find rest on that side either.

Rivka lay in her cabin, a lump of pain in her throat. She needed to come to terms with the new reality that had been forced upon her. Menachem had his own life and was doing well, she told herself. Still, a small and private insult lived somewhere in the depths of her soul: He forgot about her and moved on. But why, for God's sake, of all the women in the world did he choose her daughter?! Was God punishing her for giving herself to the Nazi? Or for not rescuing her parents? Or maybe because she didn't go with them to the afterlife? That might have been the best solution. She tried to console herself for their loss and rejoice in finding her daughter.

At night she awoke from both nightmarish and pleasurable dreams. She tried to deny it, but it was as if she were making love with Menachem through the walls.

Rivka could not believe it when finally, she saw from far away, Lady Liberty on the horizon, her burning torch in her hand. She hoped that it symbolized her freedom from the cabin she'd been hiding in and the shackles of her passion that chained her to a man she couldn't have.

Chapter 45

Menachem's friends from work picked them up from the port and took them directly to the hotel. There were two rooms waiting for them there. Before entering their rooms, they arranged to meet for breakfast at the café across from the hotel.

Again, Menachem felt Rivka's presence through the common wall. He was tormented, and his body was overheating. He tossed and turned in bed, and when dawn approached, he finally gave up on sleep and got up to wash his face.

Rivka slept a fitful sleep full of dreams. She'd forgotten to close the bedroom curtains and, as her room faced east, she found herself awake with the first rays of the sun. She got up and walked around the room. The window called to her. She opened it, and instantly the wind entered and set the curtains to dancing in front of the awakening city.

The New York City streets, still wet with the morning dew, were already filling up with traffic and noise. The sun rose higher and higher and lit Rivka's face. She closed her eyes, trapped by the sun's rays as if she were caught in a special place where time stands still. The murmur of the awakening city brought her back to reality and the knowledge of what the day would bring.

She dressed slowly, examining the effects of time on her body in the full-length mirror, wrapping herself in clothes, and combing her beautiful hair that had faded with the years. It seemed as if an era had passed, or perhaps it was in another life that she and Menachem had shared intimacy and their hearts. She had reached a place of acceptance and filed this memory in the drawer of the distant past. She looked at the clock on the wall. She was ready.

They met at the café and ordered a rich breakfast: eggs, drinks, pancakes. The best of this land, the land of opportunities. After Menachem paid the bill, they hailed a taxi to begin their search for Laibel. Menachem got in the backseat and Rivka climbed in after him. Her scent and nearby presence stunned him. Suddenly they were alone, out of sight. She pulled her eyes away from the window and looked at him. When their eyes met, a flow of electricity passed between them. The years of yearning and the tension that had built up since they'd met on the kibbutz came down to that moment. They attacked each other with a passion devoid of any logic.

Menachem gave the driver the address of the hotel. The driver made a perfect square and dropped them off exactly where he had picked them up. They rushed up to Menachem's room, barely holding back on the way. As soon as the door opened, they fell upon each other as if they had never been apart. The exploded together like lava from a volcano. They spent the whole day and the night after in a storm of uncontrollable passion.

Everything was so familiar. Showering together and sleeping hugging each other, inseparable. They felt a sense of home.

The next morning Rivka arose with a cry that had begun in her dream. Her outburst woke Menachem, and he tried to soothe and comfort her.

"I can hardly believe this is my life." She wiped her nose. "How can it be that I longed for you all these years, and here, when we finally find each other again you are married to my daughter! My own daughter! How could I look her in the eye? How can I look into Walter's eyes, when out of love he sent me on this trip, unknowing, into your arms?"

She reached for a handkerchief that Menachem gave her. "I betrayed you with Walter, you betrayed me with my daughter, I betrayed my daughter with you, and I made you betray your wife ..."

Menachem tried to calm her down, stroking her, hugging her, and kissing her. Rivka slowly quieted, melting into his touch, addicted to the absolute present. She felt that with every kiss, a concern melted and evaporated, at least for the time being.

She spoiled him with the caresses that he loved. She ran her fingers gently over his throat, legs, buttocks, the back of his neck, and behind his ears. Menachem couldn't stop moaning with pleasure. They made love again, followed by another shower. As they dressed, they began to feel embarrassment at their behavior. They decided they should take a break to digest what they'd done. They still went down together for dinner in the hotel restaurant, but when they finished, they returned to their separate rooms. They would meet the next morning to plan where they would look for Laibel and what they would say to him when they found him.

Chapter 46

Menachem's beard had grown on the trans-Atlantic voyage. Wearing his yarmulke, he started to rub shoulders with the yeshiva students in the kosher restaurants in the orthodox neighborhood in Brooklyn. It was the best starting point could he think of. He bought a bagel with lox and sat down at one of the seats at the counter.

"*Shalom aleichem,*" said the guy with *peyes* and *tallis* next to him.

Menachem smiled and raised his coffee cup in a toast. "*Aleichem shalom,*" replied Menachem.

"Where are you from?" the young man asked, curious about his looks, which seemed to be from another place.

"*Yisrael,*" said Menachem and continued eating his bagel. "Maybe you know where I can pray here? I was actually looking for someone to ask since I'm new to the area."

The young man smiled and invited him to join the *minyan* in the prayer at the nearby synagogue. Menachem accepted the invitation and the next day he took a taxi to the address he was given. The synagogue was large and luxurious, and it reminded him more of a church because it was totally different and not as modest as the synagogues he was familiar with in Israel. He took a prayer book and stood and prayed the evening prayer with the men gathered there. At the end of the prayer, his new friend invited him to a Sabbath meeting, to spend the weekend with his friends, and to listen to the rabbi, pray and eat. Menachem gladly agreed.

He recognized Laibel easily from Rivka's description. He sat next to Laibel at lunch and occasionally asked him for an explanation of the words of the rabbi. And when they weren't listening to the rabbi, Menachem told him stories about the young State of Israel. Laibel liked Menachem immediately.

In the meantime, Rivka spent time alone in the hotel. She had plenty of opportunity to reflect on all that had happened in recent days. She experienced waves of heat, longing, guilt, and anger. She lay on her bed staring at the ceiling. She ignored her hunger and rarely went down to eat. Her mind was a tempest of emotions, and she kept returning to the details of every minute of her time together with Menachem since they'd sat in that taxi. Sometimes a smile lit up her face, and sometimes gloomy clouds covered it and her stomach turned.

Pangs of conscience began to bother her, and she could not find peace. She realized that she had caused enough damage to her family. If she had not stayed behind in Poland and had joined her family when they went to America, perhaps everyone would have been living together happily. It is likely that

David would have not committed suicide and her husband wouldn't have become an alcoholic and died. The decision was made. She would not hurt her daughter; Rachel's marriage to Menachem would not be ruined.

Several days had passed. Menachem prayed in Laibel's synagogue regularly, three times a day. He attended more frequently than anyone else so as not to miss a chance to see Laibel whenever possible. He hoped that spending time with him would encourage a friendship. When Menachem felt that the relationship between them was close enough, he dared to ask Laibel about his family. Laibel hesitated and looked down, fiddling with his tallis. But in the end, he gave in to the temptation to share his burden, perhaps because he needed it so very much.

"I found consolation in religion," he said. "The rabbi was the only one who cared."

"Cared?" Menachem asked.

"Yes. Dad put us in boarding school; he could not raise us alone. But maybe I was lucky. This way I found my rabbi and the arms of the welcoming, sweet religion. Here, I found companionship, care, comfort, and most importantly, love for the Creator."

"And what happened to your mother?" Menachem asked gently.

"My mother stayed in Europe," he said after a long pause. "That was very painful for me." When he spoke about his mother, Laibel felt a little twinge in his heart. Despite everything, he felt a longing for her. Menachem could even sense it. "My brother, David, could not bear the pain. I believe that this, along with the sudden death of my aunt, brought him down, and he took he took his own life."

"My condolences on your brother," Menachem said woefully about Rivka's youngest son. He offered Laibel his hand, and Laibel accepted and bowed his head. Tiny tears squeezed through his closed eyelids.

Chapter 47

Menachem was next to Laibel as usual at the morning prayer. The folding of the tallis seemed to be happening in slow motion, time standing still. He prayed with great devotion. At the end of the prayer he walked outside with Laibel and stood there with him, preparing to speak.

"If it were possible to see your mother again, would you like to do so?" Menachem asked.

Laibel was taken aback by the unexpected question. His face went slightly paler and he withdrew into himself and didn't answer. Menachem let him be, and after the evening prayer, again, they stood outside together.

Menachem tried one more time. "Do you believe in fate?" Menachem felt it best to hide the fact that their meeting was not coincidental.

Laibel looked at him with blue eyes so much like his mother's, trying to stop the pain, but it was a losing battle and his tears won out. Menachem put a comforting arm around the younger man's shoulders until Laibel composed himself. They went in for the rabbi's class, and Menachem decided to let it go for the time being. After class, the students dispersed and only the two of them remained in the study room.

"What is the meaning of all these questions?" Laibel asked, concern furrowing his brow.

Menachem decided it was time to tell Laibel as much of the truth as he needed to convince Laibel of his good intentions. "During the war, I traveled a lot to Poland as an emissary of the Jewish underground. My purpose was to obtain weapons for the resistance and the Jewish state we hoped to establish. There I met your mother. She was our local intelligence agent. Her help was essential. In the films here in America they would call her a spy, nothing less. This was one of the reasons she remained in Poland and didn't come to America with you."

Menachem stopped for a second to see what effect his words were having. Laibel's eyebrows rose in surprise. His mother? A spy? An intelligence agent? The innocent housewife turned out to be a sophisticated secret operative? He recalled that his mother was a superb hostess, and always baked for visitors — pastries and sweets. He remembered his beautiful home in the suburbs of Warsaw. Thanks to her, the house was always clean and welcoming.

"When people like me arrived without warning, your mother always gave us a feeling of home away from home." Menachem added.

Laibel listened intently.

"She went through many hardships and saw her parents executed in the town square, but she survived. Your mother lives in a kibbutz in northern Israel near my sister, Leah. In fact, that is how we met again. She told me about her family's journey to America. Her longing for her children and her distress at not knowing whether they survived and where they might be, although she believed that they lived in New York."

Menachem felt that he now had Laibel's full attention and that he was thirsty for more details.

"In one of the living room conversations, your mother discovered my ties to the United States administration. Because I often travel to New York for work, she asked me to try and find her long-lost family. In fact, that is how I got to you."

There was a long silence in the room. After a little while, Menachem added cautiously, "If you're willing to meet your mother, who is very eager to see you, you will not have to travel far. She is here in New York."

He could see the excitement on Laibel's face. "I must consult a rabbi. Please let me speak with the rabbi, and I promise to give you an answer tomorrow morning."

Menachem nodded. He spent the night at the yeshiva and waited anxiously for the rabbi's answer. He spent long hours without sleep, and when he did finally drop off, it was so light and restless that it did nothing at all to refresh his weary mind. Would the long journey bear fruit? Would the rabbi try to thwart the mission fearing for Laibel's faith after his encounter with his secular family? An hour before dawn, his body gave in and he fell deeply asleep.

In the morning after breakfast, Laibel approached Menachem and began to stutter with excitement. He said the rabbi had given him a three-hour break for the meeting with his mother, after which he must return to his prayers and Torah studies.

Menachem gave Laibel the hotel address and Rivka's room number. They agreed that Laibel would go there in the afternoon.

Menachem left Laibel in Brooklyn and went to his office to get some work done. He took care of some odds and ends and then hurried to prepare Rivka for her reunion with her son. When she answered her door, he momentarily forgot what he had come to tell her. She was so beautiful, all he felt was the strong desire to hug her and bring her near to his heart.

Rivka stopped him gently. "Menachem, you are so very dear to me. Your great love saved me in difficult times. When I did not know if my family had drowned in the sea, you were my anchor. For many years you were in my nightly dreams, and oh, how I longed for you. Now, I would like to try and rebuild my family. To bring Laibel back. Rachel, my daughter, is already in Israel, with her husband — you. And my grand-children, your sweet children."

Menachem felt that every word burned him anew.

Rivka burst into tears. "I will have to gather so much strength every time I see you with Rachel. My dear daughter. I will suffer immensely knowing that I cannot be with you ever again. But I won't be able to forgive myself if I keep betraying her, and knowing that her husband is betraying her too."

A moist film came over Menachem's eyes. He did not allow himself to cry. He knew that she was right. "Will you allow me one last hug?" he asked.

Rivka and Menachem remained entwined and crying for a long time.

Laibel, so very excited about the meeting with his mother, had arrived early and now stood agitated in the hall, having heard the conversation between his mother and Menachem. He wanted to run away, but his legs didn't obey.

Menachem pulled away from Rivka and said that Laibel would arrive before long so he should leave. He stepped out of the room and saw Laibel in the corridor. It never crossed his mind that Laibel might have overheard the conversation. "Please go in. I'll leave you two alone so you can talk all you want without anyone to disturb you. We will meet later."

Menachem left the room, and Rivka was left standing frozen.

Chapter 48

Laibel approached his mother hesitantly. He was very upset. Minutes of embarrassment passed slowly, like eternity. Rivka looked at him from head to toe since she had not seen him for years. He was now a man. Wearing peyes and a *shtreimel* —a devout orthodox Jew. Rivka tried to hug him. Laibel stepped away politely. His mother attributed it to his religion and his way of life and retreated from him.

After a long pause, Laibel spoke. He spoke quietly and deliberately in order to temper his stormy soul. "Every person has a destiny in this world. I know this now even more than before. I feel that not for nothing did I walk this difficult path. Not for nothing did I shut myself off from the rest of the world and devote myself to my religion and the study of the Torah."

"Do you know your life's purpose?" Rivka asked, her whole body trying to deal with the foreign, cold winds that issued from her son, her flesh.

"To save you from yourself," he answered without hesitation.

The statement hit her like an arrow. She tried to understand what he meant.

Laibel was silent for a long while, contemplating how to put his feelings into words. "I was early for our meeting. I was so excited that I couldn't wait any longer. Without wanting to I heard your conversation with Menachem."

Rivka did not move. Her eyes widened.

"I understood from that conversation that you had an affair in Poland, during the war. And even after he married Rachel, your own daughter, and they had children, you couldn't forget and once again resumed your intimacy."

Rivka blushed, gasped, and finally burst into tears. When she could speak calmly, she told him how she met Menachem. "I was left alone with your grandparents. They were very old. When I thought that you had all drowned, and my longing for you was unbearable, he appeared in my life and encouraged me to keep living and restored my hope." She told him about the collective execution of all the Jews from the neighborhood and how David's dog, Rex, saved her life.

Laibel listened intently. "Apparently, it is my fate to bring you back to the right path. For you to live the future at peace with yourself and your beloveds. Only the three of us are left from the family. Me, you, and Rachel, who has a family with Menachem and their two sons."

Rivka stared at him and was amazed by how much her son had matured.

"I am ready to help you, but in my own way, to take

responsibility for your actions and return to God." He looked Rivka directly in the eye and continued. "I am willing to go with you to Israel. Your affair with Menachem will be kept secret, and we won't reveal it to Rachel. But only under the condition that you join me in my world. I can enter one of the yeshivas in Jerusalem, and I'm sure I could get you a job there, as a housekeeper, or a cook."

"Laibel, my dear son, how you've grown. You're a man now. And your conscience guides you in the right ways. In Israel I have a partner waiting for me, and in fact he is the one who encouraged me to come to America to find you. He has been with me patiently all these years when I did not know where you were. After experiencing what the Jews went through during the war, his faith was compromised. I do not think he will be willing to suddenly convert from his secular lifestyle to a life of devotion. Walter is important to me and I want to grow old with him," Rivka said at once.

"If you are important to him, he will walk with you to a new future, even if he does not know the real reason for the change." Laibel stopped and gave his mother time to process what he just said. "You cannot refuse the proposal, but your way in the future will be a path of suffering and mental affliction, knowing that you betrayed your daughter. I learned a lot after David's suicide. I saved my soul and my life when I entered the world of the Torah. And I will tell you what I have learned. He who saves a Jewish soul, saves the entire world."

Rivka was torn inside. His words made a lot of sense, but

she could not imagine sacrificing everything she knew, her way of life and perhaps even her relationships, for a life of piety.

"I see that you are divided. However, please trust that this way Rachel can continue her life with Menachem and Menachem can carry on with his life with Rachel. If you distance yourself from them, it will be easier for him, and you too, I believe. Rachel can go through life without a divorce and without losing her mother again. There are only three of us left. David is gone. Our job is not to upset the world order, but to allow it to proceed smoothly. We have already paid a high price for personal mistakes. One more small payment, and the way to salvation, peace, and quiet will open."

Chapter 49

Rivka stared with glazed eyes at her son. She was wrapped in his sweet words, excited over his willingness to save her. And honestly, she did not see any other way out of this mess. She knew what she'd feel when she saw Menachem and her daughter. It would be an unbearable reminder day after day. She remembered the anguish she'd felt on the kibbutz and now that everything had been rekindled, the agony would double.

Rivka accepted her son's proposal. Laibel joined her and Menachem when they returned to Israel. He agreed to visit the kibbutz and allow his mother to prepare for her move. The rabbi had helped him find a yeshiva similar to the one in New York. They'd received a letter stating the yeshiva would be happy to provide a job for his mother.

Rivka opened the door to her home and stood in the doorway with her suitcase in hand. Relief mixed with endless weight accompanied her every move. Walter took her luggage and hugged her tight. She felt an infinite distance.

"Walter? Do you still love me?" she asked with cloudy eyes.

"Of course! What kind of question is that?"

"Would you agree to live a life of religion with me?" she asked. "I'm about to move to a yeshiva in Jerusalem, where I will keep house and cook."

Walter looked at her as if she were speaking a foreign language. "What happened to you in New York?"

Rivka did not say a word. She walked to the bedroom and opened the closet. She packed only the modest dresses, leaving the rest behind. She made up the bed in the guest room for Laibel and didn't disturb him during prayer. Walter felt that the strange behavior of his beloved was related to her son's extreme religiosity. The next morning at dawn, Laibel and Rivka left the house. She said goodbye to the whole family. Menachem hardly dared to look at her. She walked over and hugged Walter, who stood helpless. He looked at Laibel with suppressed rage, convinced that he was the cause of this upheaval in their lives.

Rivka and Laibel departed for their new lives. Laibel integrated quickly and settled into his studies and prayers. Rivka worked hard: She cleaned, she scrubbed, she cooked and baked the best dishes just like she did in Poland, as if all the students were her children. She felt that the exertion would free her from her sins.

In the evenings, she would sit with Laibel to sip a cup of tea with lemon. At night, she would lie on her bed in cold Jerusalem and recall her life in detail as she stared at every stain and crack on the ceiling. She'd only fall asleep at dawn, imagining herself in her beloved Menachem's arms, a contented smile gracing her lips.